ONE SHILLING.

(6)

OUT ON THE WORLD

BY
GEORGE EMMETT.

LONDON.—HOGARTH HOUSE, BOUVERIE STREET, FLEET STREET, E.C.

OUT ON THE WORLD.

BY

GEORGE EMMETT,

AUTHOR OF

"*The Boys of Bircham School,*" "*Charity Joe,*" "*The Wildrake's Schooldays,*" *etc., etc., etc.*

PROFUSELY ILLUSTRATED

BY

EMINENT ARTISTS.

Publishing Office:

HOGARTH HOUSE, 32, BOUVERIE STREET, E.C.

CONTENTS.

OUT ON THE WORLD.

BY GEORGE EMMETT,

AUTHOR OF "THE BOYS OF BIRCHAM SCHOOL," "CHARITY JOE," "TOM WILDRAKE'S
SCHOOLDAYS," ETC., ETC.

MAY-DAY—A FIRST START IN LIFE.

OUT ON THE WORLD.

BY GEORGE EMMETT,

AUTHOR OF "THE BOYS OF BIRCHAM SCHOOL," "CHARITY JOB," "TOM WILDRAKE'S SCHOOLDAYS," ETC., ETC.

CHAPTER I.

THE GIPSY.

A REMARKABLE trial closed the assizes which had been held in a quaint old city in the north of England—a trial in which the prisoner told so strange a story, that for once the dwellers in the quiet old place were awakened from the usual sluggishness with which they were wont to regard the judicial assemblages convened from time to time in the massive castle.

A proud old noble—Herbert, Earl of Falconmere—had been aroused from his sleep by the midnight intrusion of a member of a gang of gipsies which had for some time taken up their quarters on a piece of waste land adjoining Falconmere Chase.

The nobleman had grappled with his unwelcome visitor, and the struggle that ensued brought a number of stout servitors to his assistance, and the gipsy was soon safely under lock and key.

Early next morning he was conveyed to the county prison, and the damning evidence of his guilty purpose was placed in the governor's hands—a small crowbar, a set of skeleton keys, a dark lantern, and a file. As may be expected, the magistrate, at the first examination fully committed the prisoner for trial, upon the charge of burglariously entering the patrician's room for the purpose of robbery ; there was a second count, that of murderously assaulting the Earl of Falconmere with intent, &c., &c.

The prisoner—a tall, handsome fellow of about thirty-six, dark as a Spaniard, and with features which, had he not been a gipsy, would have been termed classical—preserved a dogged silence during the examination, and contenting himself with giving the earl a look of fierce disdain, was led away to await his trial.

It will be easily seen that under these circumstances the prisoner's singular story had but little chance of being credited, apart from the antipathy with which his unfortu-

nate race had ever been regarded. The circumstances under which his apprehension was effected were quite sufficient to condemn him in the minds of the intelligent jury, long before the trial took place.

Whether the strange defence he made was true or not, the gipsy evidently knew that he had but little mercy to expect, for up to the last moment he refused every offer made by the tribe to provide him with counsel.

So the trial proceeded—the prisoner calm, defiant, and at times smiling at the pompous evidence of the six footmen who rushed to their employer's rescue ; but during the time the Earl of Falconmere was speaking, his large eyes gleamed with a dusky fire, and he seemed to have great difficulty in preserving the silent, watchful manner which had marked his bearing since he first came into the dock.

Many among the few who had intently listened to the trial noted that the earl never once raised his eyes towards the prisoner, and, in spite of his seeming calmness, there was a nervous twitching of the muscles of the throat and face which bespoke an agitation within.

To the judge's question respecting his guilt, the prisoner folded his arms, and in a calm, yet bitter voice replied—

"NOT GUILTY."

There was a slight stir when the clearly-spoken words rang out, and many looked towards the speaker, a half pitying, incredulous smile upon their lips.

"*Not guilty*," he repeated, " of the crime with which I am charged. That I was found in yon *murderer's* chamber I admit, but not for the purpose he has stated. You start at the word murderer ; but look towards the rich, titled scoundrel who has this day perjured his soul—behold that pallid face— does it look as though my words were true ? See ! he rises from his seat and stag——"

Here the gipsy broke into a wild laugh, and pointed with outstretched finger towards the Earl of Falconmere, who was at that moment leaving the court. Every face had mechanically turned towards the agitated old patrician, who seemed scarcely able to walk erect.

"Prisoner," the judge said, sternly, "do you understand the terrible charge which you endeavour to fix upon a man who has but done his duty in giving evidence against you?"

"Perfectly," was the calm reply; "yes, the Earl of Falconmere is a murderer, and his soul is heavy with the crime. My lords and gentlemen,"—the gipsy drew himself up and swept the sea of faces which were turned towards him as he added, solemnly—"*he has killed his only child!*"

A subdued whisper came from the excited listeners—a whisper that gradually swelled, as it was taken up from mouth to mouth, into a low cry of horror.

The gipsy saw the effect his words had produced, not only upon those who filled the hall, but upon the judge, the barristers, and the jury; he also saw an official hastily leave the court as though to detain the earl.

As the gipsy ceased speaking, the eyes of all present were turned towards the harsh, proud face of Falconmere's last earl.

He bore the scrutiny without a muscle of his features moving, and as the judge began to address the prisoner, he rose from his seat.

"Have you any witnesses," asked the judge, "in support of this most extraordinary story?"

"None, my lord."

There was a slight buzz as the high justiciary arose to pass sentence, and as the first sound fell from his lips, the faint murmur subsided, and a dead silence reigned in the vast hall.

He spoke as a man who thoroughly believed the gipsy's statements to be a tissue of falsehoods from beginning to end, and wound up the homily by sentencing Ralph Morkar to be transported beyond the seas for the term of twenty years.

The prisoner heard his sentence without betraying the least emotion, and pointing to the earl, who yet remained standing, said in calm, measured tones—

"My lord, you have done but your duty in this instance. You are safe from the vengeance of my tribe, but let yonder perjurer beware, for from this time henceforth the Zingaries will watch for an opportunity to avenge my loss."

The Earl of Falconmere heard the gipsy's words with a scornful smile upon his lips, and making a gesture with his hand to imply that his words were intended for the astonished crowd in the body of the hall, he said—

"I cannot leave this court with the knowledge that this man's improbable story has passed unchallenged. You can judge how much reliance can be placed on his statement, from the fact that my only daughter was placed in the family vault two years previous to the woman's appearance at the Abbey gates."

Then, as though he had said sufficient to clear his character from the inevitable effects of the Zingary's defence, he bowed coldly to the judge, and left the court.

The prisoner was led from the dock by two warders, and as they were passing through a passage which led to the cells the gipsy made a rapid sign to a man, whose dark features proclaimed him one of the descendants of the ancient chivalry of Egypt.

The sign, though not perceptible to the gaolers, was seen and acknowledged by the loiterer.

He watched the condemned man until the grim-looking doors closed upon his form, and then turned sadly away.

Passing the front of the prison, he beheld Earl Falconmere enter his carriage. For a moment the gipsy stood as though turned to stone, and, as he watched the carriage roll away; the veins stood out on his swarthy forehead, and from his compressed lips there came words of such dread import, that Herbert, Earl of Falconmere, would have quailed had he heard the Zingary's oath of vengeance.

CHAPTER II.
THE CAMP.

A LIGHT blue wreath of smoke rising among the trees marked the spot where the gipsies' camp was situated.

The tribe, consisting of about twenty of both sexes, were grouped around a cauldron, from which came a powerful odour, sufficient to impregnate the air for some distance from the blazing wood fire.

Except a boy of about thirteen summers, the group were all characterized by the dark olive complexion and black elf-like locks which distinguish the wanderers to this day.

The men were, with one exception, young and lithe of limb, and the women were remarkable for their lustrous laughing eyes and white gleaming teeth.

The boy, though somewhat tanned by exposure to the sun, had that unmistakable fairness of skin which proclaimed him a stranger in blood to the dusky group by which he was surrounded. His hair, though long, and matted together from neglect, was of the richest brown, and falling in wild profusion over his handsome, well-set head, added rather than detracted from his beauty.

The boy was reclining at the feet of a venerable man, whose snow-white beard formed a strange contrast to his swarthy countenance and black fiery eyes.

The group were evidently expecting a visitor to the encampment, for, from time to time, several raised their heads and listened anxiously.

A tread suddenly broke the spell, and the aged chief, as he looked in the direction of the quick footfall, heaved a deep sigh.

"It is he," he said; "we shall now learn the worst."

As the last word left the venerable gipsy's lips, the man who had exchanged signals with Ralph strode hurriedly to the centre of the silent, expectant group.

The eagerness with which they thirsted for his intelligence was perceptible upon every face; but, faithful to the laws which forbid curiosity to any of their race, none spoke.

The new-comer fixed his dark eyes for a moment upon the fair-skinned boy, then turned abruptly towards the group of women, and as the wistful, anguished face of Ralph's wife became opposite to him, his lips twitched nervously, and the words he was about to utter died away upon his tongue.

As though ashamed of this weakness, he set his teeth firmly, and in a low, but perfectly audible voice, said, in the strange, figurative language of their Eastern forefathers—

"Not until the swallows have crossed the seas, or the earth has worn a white pall twice ten years, will the wanderer return to his tribe; neither in the noon of day nor under the black pall of night will he come, until twenty long winters have passed and gone."

Save the stifled shriek of agony that came from Ralph's wife, no sound came from the gipsies when this intelligence was made known; but the dusky fire that shone in their dark eyes told how deeply they felt the fate which had befallen their companion.

The old chief arose, and pointing upward to the vaulted canopy of heaven, said, in solemn, impressive tones—

"In gloom, in sunlight, in sleeping or waking, and until Azrael, the angel of death, hovers over him with her dark wings—until then may the doer of this evil be accursed!"

From the angry group came in deep, savage accents—

"May he be accursed!"

The gipsy chief raised his head, and making a silent gesture towards the women, they arose and meekly left the spot, taking with them the beautiful fair-skinned boy.

"Now," the old chief said, "we will hear the black lies which have this day robbed me of a son, and you of a companion."

The man who had brought the intelligence of Ralph's doom inclined his head in token of assent, then seating himself near the cheerful fire, he related all that had passed in the hall of justice.

They listened with grave attention, and at the conclusion of the recital the old chief discontinuing the figurative mode of speech which had hitherto embellished his words said—

"To-morrow messengers must be sent through the whole length and breadth of the land, that the district chiefs may search for the clue to substantiate the story Ralph this day told before those wise men of England. The knife would be a quicker mode of revenge, but it would not enrich the boy who has eaten of our bread. Once a proof of the boy's birth and relationship in our possession, then Herbert, Lord of Falconmere, dies, and the outcast shall reign in his stead."

"Until the clue is found," asked Tinker Tom, "is Falconmere to rest in peace while he we love so well drags out a dreary life in the convict settlement?"

"It must be so; but stay. What were his wishes? You spoke by signs before he was led away."

"None. He bid me take care of the boy. No more passed between us."

"Are you willing to do so?"

Tinker Tom mused for a moment, then raising his head, he answered—

"I am. More so, since he can become an instrument in my plan of vengeance."

"Ah! How so? Remember the boy is to be kept sacred from harm."

"No harm shall befall him," said Tinker Tom. "Have I your permission to unfold my plan?"

The chief bowed his kingly head.

"There is but one being in the world whom this stern noble loves," said the stalwart gipsy; "that one a blue-eyed child whom he has adopted. To lose her would bring a deep sorrow upon his heart, and, in part, avenge the loss we have this day suffered."

He paused, that his words might have weight with the silent group whose permission would have to be obtained before he could begin his well-defined plot against the lordly owner of Falconmere.

"With the boy's aid," he resumed, "it will be an easy matter to lure her from the Abbey grounds. Once in my possession," the gipsy added, vindictively, "she shall be reared as a beggar. In the hands of an old thief-trainer she will become a fitting tool for my purpose."

The gipsy chief pondered long over these words before he said—

"Under the supposition that the girl has

become all you would make her, in what manner do you intend to use her *talents?* Is it against the earl, who has reared her from her infancy with a father's love?"

"It is," said Tinker Tom, his eyes aglare at the thought of his plan of vengeance. "Her degradation shall be the means of crushing the earl's pride. In the same spot that Ralph stood this day will I bring the earl's *protégée*, and he—her adopted father—shall give such evidence against her that will brand her with the convict's mark for ever; and when the final doom is passed, and not till then, will he know that the fair-haired child who has so oft nestled at his breast and the condemned convict are one."

The vindictive spirit that prompted this subtle revenge cared not for the time that must elapse ere he could strike this crushing blow upon the lordly owner of Falconmere.

"We have heard you," said the chief, looking towards the swarthy group; "let the tribe say if your plan is good."

The men were silent, and Tinker Tom, who knew the ominous sign, bit his lip until the blood came slowly from the punctured skin.

"Does my plan seem too long for the anger that is in your hearts?" he asked, turning to the tribe. "Think you that the knife would be a fitter mode of revenge?"

"We do," they answered. "It is too long to wait. Years must elapse before the first blow is struck."

"Ay," Tinker Tom said; "years must elapse. Every year will be an age of sorrow for the man who has so deeply wronged us. Know you not that his love for this child is the only sign of human feeling he has shown since he drove his daughter to a suicide's grave? Picture the old man in his loneliness, waiting daily, hourly, for the return of the object of his love. Behold him when the child he has so long mourned has budded into womanhood—rich, possibly, in outward beauty, but her heart blackened by evil—a thief, a felon. Fill up the picture by the knowledge being suddenly imparted to him that the sweet child he nurtured has fallen so low that she steals into her childhood's home and robs the sorrow-stricken being who has so long mourned her loss—think of this, and tell me, is the vengeance, though tardy, worth waiting for?"

The impassioned manner in which he spoke, the facial changes which accompanied every word, the fiendish delight with which he portrayed the earl's sorrow, had their weight, and a low buzz of admiration came from the assembly.

There was one whose thirst for immediate vengeance could not be appeased. He claimed a closer kindred with the condemned man than any who sat by the blazing camp fire.

Ralph Morkar had married this man's sister, and Black Moreau's fierce longing for the earl's life could ill brook the subtle schemes set forth by Tinker Tom.

He arose when the latter had ceased speaking, and pointed towards the huts where the women of the tribe could be seen grouped around the bereaved young wife, who looked upon the doom that had that day fallen upon her husband as an eternal separation.

"Look!" Moreau said, passionately; "think you yon weeping woman can wait the long years your plan will take to develope? Think you that the knowledge of a coming vengeance will soothe her lacerated heart when her mind travels to that far-off land where her husband toils, with an accursed chain impeding every movement of those limbs that have been hitherto as free as the air we breathe? It is her we should consult in this great wrong—it is her voice that has said 'Give the evil-doer's body to the knife, and level his proud walls to the ground.' What say you, my friends? Shall it be so?"

To this excited harangue Tinker Tom replied with all the arguments he had previously used. To them he added the danger that would accrue from slaying the Earl of Falconmere—a danger he showed them that would, in all probability, end with the extermination of the tribe.

"In part, Moreau," he said, in conclusion, "your wishes may be met. We will fire the Abbey, and under cover of the flames I will obtain possession of those papers which have caused your kinsman to be taken from among us."

Moreau heard him patiently—his dark eyes glaring with a savage light, and his white teeth gleaming between his parted lips, gave the stern, passion-worked features a demon-like expression.

"And the earl?" he asked; "is he to perish in the flames?"

"That," Tinker Tom said, "must be left to chance. The Abbey fired, the girl and the papers in my possession, we can be content for a while."

The venerable chief would fain have altered the cruel work; but for once his words were without authority, and sighing deeply, he arose, and left the angry, fierce-looking group to mature their plans of vengeance.

CHAPTER III.

LATOUR AND THE EARL.

EARL FALCONMERE'S body-servant was a Frenchman by birth, cunning and unscrupulous by nature, gaunt in form, and cadaverous in features.

His step was as soft and as stealthy as a cat's, and the small bead-like eyes seemed always peering and prying into the countenances of all he met, as though endeavouring to read the inmost thoughts and feelings of those who had the high honour of Monsieur Jules Latour's acquaintance.

There was none, save the earl, in the princely establishment who had a good word for the French valet. From the stable-boy to the pompous steward, one and all hated the soft, sneaking, cat-like gentleman who honoured the Abbey with his presence.

He seemed to possess an unlimited sway with the earl, and though his foes sought to shake the nobleman's confidence in his valet's fidelity, they signally failed.

That a secret of momentous import was in the valet's possession, the *ladies* and *gentlemen* in the servants' hall devoutly believed.

There seemed some truth in their belief, for when the earl returned from the trial he was followed into his study by the gaunt Frenchman.

There was a peculiar expression upon the valet's saturnine countenance as he glided behind his master—a mingled look of hate and triumph, so blended that it was impossible to tell which feeling predominated.

As noiseless as a shadow Latour passed inside the chamber; then carefully closing the door, he placed his back against it, and said—

"Is he put out of the way?"

The earl, whose haughty features now looked pale and careworn, sank into his chair, and briefly answered—

"Transported for twenty years."

"Good!" said the valet; "he will not trouble your lordship again."

"Personally he will not," said Earl Falconmere; "but the tribe, or I am much mistaken, will seek a terrible revenge for the punishment their companion has this day received."

"Does your lordship fear the vagrants?"

Latour's thin lips wore the faintest possible expression of scorn as he asked this question.

"Fear them?" the earl said, angrily; "I fear no man, face to face, but I am powerless to cope with a score of cunning vagabonds who would use secret assassination as a retaliation for what has transpired."

Latour rubbed his hands softly, and his voice sounded more like the purring of a cat than aught else.

"My lord is sure," he said, "of the devotion I feel towards his person. If my lord fears a visit from a midnight assassin, we will, with your lordship's permission, exchange sleeping rooms."

Earl Falconmere looked at the gaunt figure before him, then glanced at his own massive and powerful limbs.

"By this proposition," he said, with a slight laugh, "it would appear you are better able to cope with an unwelcome visitor than I am."

Latour saw the look, and divined its meaning, and still softly rubbing his hands, he answered in a low hissing voice—

"In strength, my lord, I am but a child, but in cunning I could owtwit even the serpent. Will my lord suffer me to occupy his room to-night?"—he showed his discoloured teeth as he added—"it will be both prudent and wise. Your lordship rarely finds Latour's advice a matter of regret after."

The earl paused for a moment, then raising his eyes, which had hitherto been fixed upon the carpet, he looked steadily at the Frenchman's immovable countenance.

"I thank you," he said, "for this proof of your devotion, but as we shall leave the Abbey in a few days, I think the change will be unnecessary."

Latour bowed, and was about to leave the room; his hand was upon the door-handle when the earl's voice arrested him.

"By the way, Latour," he said, "have you visited the vault since—since the Lady Alice was buried?"

"I have not, my lord."

The earl again began to study the pattern of the carpet, and after playing with his watch-chain for a few seconds, he said—

"Do so. That fellow's story I have every reason to believe made an impression upon the jury; and should there be an inquiry, and, perhaps, an investigation into its truth, it will be necessary to have *everything prepared.*"

"Your lordship's wishes shall be attended to forthwith."

So saying, the valet bowed and glided from the room. As he hurried down the broad staircase, an expression of baffled hate lit up his features, and from between his thin lips came the words—

"Foiled again. So he leaves the Abbey, fearful that the gipsies will wreak their vengeance upon him. So, so; this very fear may yet serve my purpose."

The earl, when Latour had closed the door, placed his elbow upon the table, and leaning his forehead upon his palm, became lost in thought.

From the many changes his face underwent, it was evident his musings were of a most painful nature. The greater part of an hour passed and he moved not, nor would he then, had not the door suddenly opened and a beautiful child of about ten summers bounded into the room.

She saw the deep grief visible upon the

earl's face, and stopping short in the centre of the apartment, she looked wistfully at the stalwart form, awed into silence by the strange wild gleam of the earl's dark lustrous eyes.

The rich sunlight, falling through the stained glass windows, cast its prismatic hues upon the child's long golden hair, playing like a halo around the sweet infantile face; and as she stood with half-averted head, one little hand raised towards the earl, her attitude was filled with that grace which painter, sculptor, or poet, would fain have imitated, but not excelled.

Finding, after a pause of several seconds' duration, that her entry had been unnoticed, she approached the earl, her foot falling as lightly as snow falls to the ground.

He felt the gentle touch of her soft delicate hand upon his arm, and looking up, beheld the child's blue eyes fixed upon him with a sad, enquiring glance.

There was no tie of blood between them, but he had been as a sire to the fatherless orphan, and she repaid this kindness by loving her benefactor with all the fervency of her affectionate nature.

"Little one," he said, "tell me what you have done since I went away this morning."

The little arms were twined around his neck, and the soft damask cheek was placed fondly against his as she answered—

"I had my music lesson, papa, and read a little with governess. Then I went out with Flossy, and had such fun in the park—rare fun it was, for Flossy kept barking and jumping after the birds, and could not catch one; but I cried after that, papa."

"Cried, my darling; what caused you to cry?"

"Jack Lennox, papa."

The peer raised his eyebrows and repeated the name.

"Pray, Lily, who is Jack Lennox? one of the grooms?"

"No, papa; he is a poor little gipsy."

The peer started, and instinctively drew the fair child close to his breast.

"A gipsy," he said, gravely; "surely my darling does not seek a playmate among the wandering vagrants who infest the wood."

"No, papa; but poor Jack is not a gipsy, he says, and I don't think he is, because he is not so dark as that horrid man that came once, and had a fire hanging to the handle of —a—a machine, I think that sulky Latour called it."

She paused, as though trying to recollect the explanation given by Latour of the various uses to which Tinker Tom put his knife-grinding machine, and the earl, who had been held spell-bound by her words,

waited with bated breath for her to resume her childish explanation.

"There," she said, "I have forgotten all about it. But poor little Jack Lennox, papa—I'm sure you would give him a pair of shoes. I wish my old ones would fit him; but they—"

"Yes, darling, I will give him a pair; but what were you saying about the boy not being a gipsy?"

"Oh, I asked him one day."

"One day?"

"Yes, papa; he often comes in the park when I am playing with Flossy. Poor little fellow, he did cry so, to-day; he made me feel so sad that I was obliged to cry as well."

The earl frowned angrily, as he said—

"You have not told me the question you asked him yet, darling."

"No, papa; I will. One day I asked him why he was not so dark as the men and women I had seen in the wood, and he told me that he was not a gipsy. He said he had no papa or mamma, and when he was very little the gipsies found him in a wood, and have been kind to him ever since; but I don't think they can be kind, because he has no shoes to wear; do you think so, papa?"

The earl did not answer; his face was now as white as a sheeted corpse, and his lips moved in that nervous, twitching manner which showed how deeply he struggled with the pent-up feeling in his breast.

"When I saw him to-day," the child went on, "he told me that the gipsy who had been so kind to him had been taken away; and he cried so—— What is the matter, papa?"

A deep groan had escaped the earl's lips in spite of every effort, and the alarmed child, kissing the ghastly face, said anxiously—

"You look ill, papa. Shall I call Latour?"

"No, no, my darling; I am better now. Run to your governess, and get ready for your afternoon drive; and mind, Lily, you never go in the wood again alone."

"I will not, papa, if you do not wish it."

"I do not, darling. Kiss me—here comes Latour. There, come to me after you have finished your afternoon lesson."

As the child left the earl's side, Latour entered the chamber.

"*Everything is ready*, my lord," he said. "should your fears be realized."

The earl inclined his head; then passing his hand across his brow to wipe away the big drops which had gathered thickly during Lily's prattle, he said—

"You wished me to exchange rooms with you, Latour. I accept your offer. How far is your chamber from Miss Lily's?"

"Directly opposite, my lord."

"Good. Place my pistols upon the table

8

before I retire, and see that the fastenings of the young lady's windows are secure."

CHAPTER IV.

MONSIEUR JULES LATOUR'S PROSPECTIVE FORTUNE.

By degrees the lights in the various chambers in Falconmere Abbey were extinguished, and all, save two, who dwelt within the sombre pile, were paying tribute to the drowsy god of night.

The earl and his valet had exchanged sleeping apartments, and though midnight had long since chimed, neither had sought repose.

In the valet's chamber the lamp had long been turned down, and in the silent gloom sat the peer, one hand supporting his throbbing brow, the other nervously clutching the butt of an exquisitely mounted pistol.

The wind, as it came sighing among the ivy, and sweeping around the quaint gables in fitful gusts, seemed to the lonely watcher like the footfall of a prowling marauder.

Time after time he arose, and hastily opened the chamber door, and sought to pierce the deep gloom in the long corridor; then the wind would lull, and the silent, determined man, after listening to the little Lily's gentle respiration, walked moodily to his seat, and resumed his lonely vigil.

So passed the night with Falconmere's proud earl, and when the sunbeams stole through the window, they played upon a face older by ten years in appearance to what it looked when the rosy light gladdened the earth on the previous morn.

His eyes were wild and bloodshot, the features pinched and careworn, and his lips, though tightly compressed, wore the hue of one who had passed to another world.

There must have been a greater cause than his anxiety for the gentle child's safety to have worked this wondrous change.

In the darkness of that long night the memory of a great wrong perpetrated by the stern, pitiless man came strong upon him; the murky air seemed filled with strange shapes, and a low, wailing cry was ever ringing its mournful cadence in his ear.

He knew that the white shimmering forms, and the touching voice, were but the unreal creations of his brain; yet the strange spell that came over his faculties was none the less terrible, nor his sufferings the lighter, by the oft-repeated defiant words by which he tried to dispel the shadowy terrors that weighed so heavily upon his soul.

"The dead," he would mutter, fiercely, "never return; these gleaming forms, and that wailing cry, are but the result of this day's undue excitement."

So he argued, mentally, yet his eyes, starting from their sockets, would follow the white, transparent shadow, as it floated through the darkness, and large beads of perspiration, cold and clammy, stood out upon his forehead, as the fancied cry of hopeless anguish smote, from time to time, upon his brain.

He would have struck a light, but the spell was too strong upon him. He dared not move from his seat nor turn his head, for the wretched man felt a cold hand placed upon his shoulder. Though it seemed but small and fair, yet the weight kept him down, and rendered his limbs incapable of movement.

With the gladsome light these strange and terrible fancies departed, and as he buried his face in his hands, a deep groan of agony welled up from his heart, and the strong man's frame trembled like one stricken with the palsy. When he arose from this position, he walked to the casement, and, throwing back the long windows, found relief in the cool morning air, as it played around his burning brow.

"Not for the sea's worth," he said, "would I pass another night like this. Yes," he added, musingly, "conscience does indeed make cowards of us all."

Long he stood gazing mechanically at the rich prospect which the sun's mellow tints were rapidly disclosing. To the east tracts of golden grain stood out in bold contrast with the rich emerald tints of the grass-covered fields, and the sombre hue of various patches of newly-ploughed earth.

The darker shades of the hedgerows which divided the fields looked not unlike the boundary marks upon a large map.

The eye, wandering beyond this, beheld a pleasing extent of undulating country, and the tiny white dwellings, nestling among clumps of tall trees, or half hidden in a sequestered valley, gave a peaceful charm to the scene.

Looking southward, the thick foliage of Falconmere Park shut out the distant view, and as the earl watched the tree-tops bend before the gentle breeze, a deep curse came from his lips, and the face—hitherto so pregnant with remorse, became distorted with passion.

A thin spiral column of smoke rising from behind the thick wood, showed where the gipsies' camp was situate. The sight aroused all that was evil in the earl's nature, and he stood glaring like a demon at the light blue cloud which gradually melted away.

As he stood thus a gentle tap at the door caused him to start, and look towards the weapons which lay upon the table.

The tap was repeated, and then Latour's well-known smooth accents were heard.

"Enter," the earl said, smoothing his disordered hair, and striving to repress his agitation.

With his usual cat-like gait the valet stole inside the chamber, and, glancing furtively at the earl, he began rubbing his hands softly, and asked—

"Has my lord slept well?"

"No, Latour," was the answer; "overanxiety has kept me awake the whole night."

Latour was grieved—deeply grieved—that such had been the case, and offered to prepare the earl a cup of coffee. The servants not yet being awake, the slimy valet would, upon such an occasion as this, soil his spotless hands.

The offer was accepted, and the earl, taking the case of pistols under his arm, retired to his own chamber.

He saw by the appearance of the bed that Latour had not slept therein. A large wrapper, lying in a careless manner upon the antique sofa, showed where the valet had passed the night. Nothing else, to all appearance, had been disturbed, although the early part of the night had been passed in a strange manner by the crafty, treacherous Frenchman.

When Latour entered the earl's chamber he extinguished the lamp, which stood upon a table near the bed. This done, he took a small lantern from beneath a loose wrapper he carried, and withdrawing the shade by which it was darkened, began to search carefully among the miscellaneous articles upon the dressing-table.

Though absorbed in this occupation, he took especial care that the circular gleam of light should not rest upon the window.

"*Peste!*" he muttered. "It is not here."

And turning from the table, he searched the pockets of the clothes the earl had that day worn. Inside the breast of a light overcoat he found the object of his search, and his saturnine countenance glowed with triumph.

It was a small key of peculiar construction and elaborate workmanship, and as the valet held it before the light, he muttered, joyfully—

"At last—at last is my patience rewarded. Month after month, year after year have I tried to obtain this key. Ha, ha! he has slept with it beneath his pillow every night for nine long years. His first waking thought has been to place it safely about his body, but once, my lord of Falconmere, your caution has left you, and Latour has profited by the omission."

To ensure against the earl's sudden entry into the chamber, he locked the door, then wheeled the sofa across, and in such a manner that the high back rose far above the keyhole.

"My lord might return," he thought, "and finding the door locked, would put his eye to the keyhole. This will make all safe so far. Now for the prize."

The key opened a large oaken chest which stood in a recess near the head of Earl Falconmere's couch. To judge by the external appearance of this massive article, every precaution had been taken to render it impregnable. There was not a square inch of the wood visible. A double row of wrought-iron plates defended the edges, and the flat surface was covered by a thick sheet of the same metal.

The key was not above two inches long, but the openings in the upper part were of such minute and peculiar make that the most skilful whitesmith would have been baffled to have picked the lock.

When Latour placed the key in the small opening he paused before turning it, and as a cunning twinkle shone in his eyes, he muttered—

"There are such things as pistol-barrels fitted to these boxes. I must be careful."

Placing the lantern upon the floor, he arose and went to the fireplace and brought the tongs. Then, keeping well away from the front of the chest, he gripped the key with the points, and, raising his hand upwards, the faint click of the lock sounded in his ears.

Latour paused for a moment as though in expectation of beholding the lid open, and hearing the sharp report of firearms.

Neither occurred; and the valet, releasing the key, applied the tongs to the rim of the lid. An expression of disappointment came over his face when he found the lid immovable.

But an instant's reflection told him that the iron plates and cover would be sufficient to cause this. Fearful that he should be unable to attain his wish, Latour, reckless of the consequences, seized the lid and threw it upwards.

Save a dull thud, which was caused by the iron rim striking the wall, there came no sound to alarm the excited Frenchman.

So with a glad cry he turned the light of his lamp upon the contents and began his search.

There was nothing in the appearance of the discoloured rolls of paper, old letters, and a few sheets of closely-written parchment, to need this secure receptacle; and as the valet took out each article, and after a careful examination placed them on the floor, his face underwent many varying expressions.

At times, when his fingers clutched a roll

of paper, his eyes would light up with exultant triumph; then, as he found they were not those he sought, the expression would change to one of blank disappointment.

So he continued until the box was nearly emptied; then in a corner, hidden by a number of old letters which had been thrown in loosely, he came upon the object of his eager search.

It was a small bundle of somewhat discoloured paper, the edges frayed, and the exterior bearing the appearance of having been long carried about in a pocket.

The small roll was tied with a piece of faded blue ribbon, and on the outside, written in the earl's bold hand, was the single word ALICIA!

Latour's fingers trembled with joy when he untied the ribbon, and, carefully opening the packet, he took therefrom a plain gold ring, two parchment certificates, and a long silken tress of sunny hair.

These he laid aside during the examination of the various letters. When this was concluded, he took the outer sheet away, and, with a roll of paper he had brought with him, made up a packet similar in size to that which he had opened.

The outer sheet he found was blank, save for the word written by the Earl of Falconmere. This he placed around the fictitious roll, then tying it with the ribbon, placed it on the carpet.

He then rolled the original, and, holding one in each hand, compared the appearance they presented.

In size they were as much alike as possible, but the edges wore quite a different aspect.

Latour opened the lantern, and pricked up the wick with the point of a penknife until it began to smoke.

Over this he held the ends of the packet he had brought to substitute for that in the earl's possession, and, as he proceeded in his cunning work, he held the soiled papers close to the light, until the new, smooth edges of the second packet became of the same hue as the old.

This done, he carefully frayed the ends with the point of his penknife; then again holding each end over the black smoke, finished his task.

He had succeeded in every way—the false roll of paper bore such a close resemblance to the original, that, unless they were opened, detection was impossible.

As he carefully replaced the contents of the oblong box, Latour's lips parted, and a low chuckle of triumph, mingled with expressions of peculiar import, broke from him.

When the task was finished he carefully closed the box, locked it, and replaced the key in the breast-pocket of the earl's overcoat.

This done, he gathered the abstracted letters, and putting the certificates and ring into a pocket-book, arose from the ground and went to the sofa.

Here, stretched at full length, he read the contents of the packet, and by the time he had concluded, the first streak of day began to struggle through the darkness.

The reading seemed satisfactory, for Latour placed the papers in an inside pocket and mused—

"So, by a codicil added to her uncle's will, Greyford, with its rent-roll of four thousand, was hers; in the event of her death, to pass to the boy, if they were lawfully married. They were. Well, in the event of the boy's death it passes to the earl. Ah! I begin to see a little clearer now. Yes, the earl is the happy possessor of this snug little windfall; but whether he will long possess it remains at the discretion of Monsieur Jules Latour, *valet de chambre* to the Earl of Falconmere."

Latour closed his eyes and pondered over the knowledge he had achieved. He had no particular dislike towards his employer; but when he maturely deliberated over the affair, he came to the conclusion that it would be more chivalrous to befriend a homeless boy than to accept a heavy bribe from the earl to keep the secret.

"Besides," he mentally argued, "the boy will feel grateful to me for the interest I feel in his behalf, and he cannot do less than give me, his only friend and guardian, a thousand a year to sustain that important and very respectable position."

He became so excited with this prospect, that he almost believed he had achieved the distinction and emolument he had marked out for himself.

When he had sufficiently indulged his fancies with this pleasant prospect, his mind again reverted to the mode of attainment.

"I wonder," he soliloquized, "how such a wary, careful man as this master of mine appears in all his transactions, should have kept the letter from the lawyer announcing the sudden change in the old curmudgeon's sentiments towards his fair niece. Let me see. The old fellow was the lady's mother's brother. Exactly; and with him the last of the name passed away. Let me see."

He drew the packet from his pocket, and selecting a letter written in the unmistakable caligraphy of a lawyer's clerk, read the concluding paragraph.

Having done so, the paper was replaced, and put carefully away.

"Yes," Monsieur Jules Latour resumed,

"should everything be correct respecting the boy's parentage, he takes the old family name and the money to support it. Now, I think the first step will be to secure the will, if it is in the box. I think my best plan will be to take it, and then take myself off."

Monsieur Jules laughed at his little joke as he rose from the sofa and crossed the room. He was in such a genial mood with himself that he could have laughed at the merest trifle.

When he found the will he not only laughed, but capered about the room with a buoyancy that would have excited envy among the dancing dervishes of the beautiful but dirty city of the Sultan.

Monsieur Jules returned to the sofa after restoring the key to its place, and opening the lining of his coat, placed the will inside.

"The will, the certificate of marriage, also of the boy's baptism, in my possession," he said, gleefully, "I think the thousand a year much nearer than it was an hour since."

He left off to rub his hands, and so energetically was this process carried out that the flesh became the colour of beet-root.

"Now to find the boy," he resumed, when his fingers tingled with pain; "then, if possible, to obtain the clothes he wore that night; but that will not be a very difficult affair if the gipsy spoke the truth yesterday. If the clothes are not obtainable, there is a mark upon the boy's body, at least, so the unfortunate lady states. Well, I shall see about this soon. Now I think the mode of operation pretty well laid out. Should—ah! why not?—If this is not the rightful heir, I must find one; that will be very easy. As for the earl, I think the little secret connected with the family vault will cause him to keep the peace towards my very excellent self. Monsieur Jules Latour, you can commence your thousand a year from to-day."

He laughed so heartily at this that the tears came to his eyes, and a severe pain cramped his right side.

"Laughing does not agree with my tender frame," commented Monsieur Jules, as he tenderly rubbed his side. "I must be careful, and make a note of that. Now for the earl. I wonder how he has slept while I have been making a fortune?"

By the time Monsieur Jules reached the earl's presence all traces of the late hilarity had passed away from his features, and he seemed the quiet, attentive servant of yore.

And when he brought the earl the promised coffee, he gently persuaded the nobleman to take a few hours' rest now that all danger was past.

The earl yielded to the advice, and while he slept Monsieur Jules was busy in his own chamber packing a leather valise ready for his contemplated flight.

Monsieur Jules, before placing the most useful articles of clothing in the valise, carefully unfastened one side of the internal canvas covering, then between that and the bottom he spread the precious papers.

A little glue refastened the canvas, and, as Monsieur Latour remarked, when rubbing his hands—

"No one would suspect that anything was hidden there."

Long before the earl rang for his valet the preparations were complete, and Latour waited but for the opportunity to visit the gipsies before he bade an eternal farewell to Falconmere Abbey.

If there is any truth in the story told by the gipsy, and in Latour's musings, our ragged little hero is the grandson of an earl, and the heir to a fortune.

We must leave the solution to that grim old tyrant, Time, and the *disinterested* kindness of Monsieur Jules Latour.

CHAPTER V.
THE ABDUCTION.

No servant could have been more attentive in the discharge of his duties than Latour appeared when in attendance upon the earl that morning; he assisted the nobleman to dress for a hunt that was to take place that day, and while handing him his velvet hunting-cap he made a suggestion to the nobleman which met with the warmest approval.

"I have been thinking, my lord," he said, "that the men, as a rule, are not fitting companions for Miss Lily during her rambles in the park or the adjacent forest."

The earl looked enquiringly at his valet, then turned to the glass to finish the arrangement of his neckcloth.

"I have had much to do with children," Latour continued, "before I had the honour of entering your lordship's service—(This was true; the rascal had a wife and family residing in a low suburb of Paris, deserted and destitute)—therefore I know the difficulty that exists at times in answering their questions."

The earl gave an impatient stamp with his foot.

"Yes, yes; I understand," he said. "You think the grooms would, in consequence of their ignorance, be unable to answer a simple question Miss Lily's inquiring mind might suggest."

"Precisely so, my lord; therefore, with your permission, I will accompany the young lady upon her morning walk."

The permission was readily granted, and as the earl rode away from the Abbey, Latour watched him from the window, his face anything but expressive of the deferential mask he had so well worn during his attendance upon his master

The reason Latour had made this offer was the result of a long debate with himself.

He wished to confer with one of the gipsies, also to make the acquaintance of the boy he felt so keen an interest in advancing.

By judiciously placing his ear to the key-hole he had overheard the conversation between the beautiful child and her benefactor. He had no particular reason at the time for doing this; it was merely the result of a confirmed habit—a passion if you like. Monsieur Jules could not pass a door when two persons inside were conversing.

He had a theory that, sooner or later, such a mode of proceeding must result in obtaining information that would be useful, though, to speak the truth, the little items of conversation he had overheard in the pantry and the housekeeper's room had not realised this theory; far from it, he had often listened to the most scurrilous adjectives coupled with his own name from those chambers, and had been compelled to retire in consequence.

He heard the earl and the child speaking as he glided down the long corridor, and every word she had uttered flashed across his brain when he perused the packet of letters.

With Lily's guidance, he had no doubt of soon finding the boy she knew by the name of Jack Lennox.

Besides, as Monsieur Jules argued, it would not be prudent to be seen by any of the male domestics as he went in search of the gipsies. Under these circumstances his generous offer served two purposes—one to obtain speech with the boy, the other to approach the camp without being seen.

The latter he deemed necessary, not knowing how many days might elapse before he brought his negotiations to a satisfactory conclusion with the gipsy who had so long befriended the boy, who was to aid him in the possession of a thousand a year.

Monsieur Jules rubbed his hands when he thought how well his story had become verified; and keeping up the imperceptible cleansing, he went softly towards the young lady's room to offer his valuable services as companion during her ramble.

He met the beautiful child at the wide oaken staircase. She had a small basket in her hand to hold the wild flowers which she so fondly loved to gather.

The bright blue eyes dilated with amazement when Latour told her that the earl wished him to accompany her in her morning walk.

There was a little pouting and some slight show of resistance before she would accept her gaunt escort; but when Monsieur Jules told her that her ramble in the park would be forfeited unless he accompanied her, she gave in.

"I will tell papa," she thought, as they left the Abbey, "how much I should prefer being left to myself."

She little knew that she had parted from the earl for many, many years, when she stepped forth from the grim old pile into the fresh-brilliant sunshine.

Latour was too busy with his schemes to place much constraint upon the child. At times, in eager pursuit of a bright-winged insect, she would become lost among the trees, and her guardian would have to rush in search of his precious charge.

Her happy face became clouded when he overtook her, and she would sit upon the grass revolving a childish plan to escape Latour's surveillance.

It was strange, this antipathy she felt towards the earl's valet. He had never offended the little lady in any manner, yet she shrank from his touch as she would from a venomous reptile.

"I wish," she thought, as she gazed upwards at the white fleecy clouds, "it would rain. I don't like this man to be with me, and if I thought papa would not be cross with me for returning so soon, I would go back to the Abbey."

Monsieur Jules, leaning against the trunk of a tree, was mentally wondering when it would please the little lady to wend her steps towards the forest.

He was anxious to confer with the gipsies, still more anxious to obtain, if possible, the clothes worn by the future owner of Greyford when he fell among the Zingaries.

Finding the child continued plucking the petals from a bunch of daisies she had gathered, he asked in his blandest tones—

"Would Miss Lily like to go in the forest?"

She looked pleased at this, and readily answered—

"Yes; but you must keep a long way behind, because—because——"

"I will, if mademoiselle wishes it; but why must I do so?"

He saw the child's face overspread with a rosy blush, and instantly the earl's injunction came across his mind.

"Ah!" Monsieur Jules mentally remarked, "she wishes to meet this ragged playmate of hers, and fears that I shall prevent it."

The little girl made no answer to Latour's query. She could not tell a lie, neither could she state the reason she wished Monsieur Jules to be as far as possible from her.

She had not forgotten the promise she had made the earl to hold no more meetings with

LILY SHRANK BACK AT THIS THREAT, AND CLUNG YET CLOSER TO HER COMPANION

the gipsies' *protégé*, but her heart told her it would be cruel not to see her little playmate once more, and tell him that her papa had forbidden her to meet him again.

She was thinking how this could be managed, when Latour's words solved the matter ; so, without any attempt to form an excuse for the request she had made, she rose and walked slowly towards the confines of the park.

When nearly two hundred yards from the spot where she had been sitting, she paused, and looking into Latour's face, said—

"Oh ! Monsieur Latour, I have left my basket behind—do fetch it for me."

"Certainly, mademoiselle, certainly," said the obliging schemer as he turned and began to retrace his steps. "Don't walk fast; I shall soon overtake you."

Lily watched the Frenchman until his lath-like form became lost among the trees ; then, clapping her hands with joy, she turned towards the forest, and bounded away with the fleetness of a young fawn.

Her silvery laughter pealed out as she passed through a broken portion of the high fence that enclosed the park ; then taking a path that led towards a clump of trees, she was soon lost to sight.

When Monsieur Jules Latour returned with the basket, his eyes opened wide with amazement. The little lady was gone, and though Monsieur Jules ran until he was out of breath, he failed to discover the path she had taken.

Consoling himself with the hope that he should come up with her in the forest, he passed through the fence, and began to look eagerly around.

Crouching behind a huge bushy tree, Tinker Tom and another of the tribe saw Monsieur Latour enter the forest, and as his gaunt form passed through the fence, the gipsies, quitting their place of concealment, ran swiftly in his track.

Tinker Tom's swarthy face beamed with triumph, and, drawing back the hammer of a gun he carried, he hissed between his set teeth—

"If that fellow interferes, I will put a bullet through his head."

"Do so," said his companion, "and the report of your piece will bring a dozen keepers upon us. My plan is the best and safest."

"Be it so," said Tinker Tom, lowering the hammer of his fowling-piece ; "perhaps it will be the quietest way of doing the business. Have you the rope ?"

The second gipsy held up a coil of strong cord in reply. Tinker Tom nodded, and renewed the pursuit.

Latour by this time had begun to feel alarmed at the sudden disappearance of his charge, and, running to and fro, he called her loudly by name.

Passing through a clump of trees, he came suddenly upon the gipsies' encampment. The tents were struck, and the beasts of burden laden ready for instant departure.

To his wild inquiries he received a surly answer, and was told to leave the camp.

Though in a state of wild excitement, Latour marked the aspect of the tribe, and comparing the sudden departure of the wanderers with the earl's fears, he felt assured that the young girl had fallen into their power.

This was not a matter of much moment to Monsieur Jules. He could have returned to the Abbey and escaped with his valise before the earl came home from the hunt.

So, with a forced laugh, he walked towards the venerable old chief, and was about to address him in furtherance of the design he had already formed.

Before he could utter a word, the old man waved him back, and said—

"You have been told to depart. Do so ; we desire not your presence."

"But a few words," said Latour. "I have a matter that may be of advantage to us both, if you will permit me to dis——"

Tinker Tom and his companion burst through the thicket at that moment, and, in obedience to a sign from their chief, seized Latour and hurried him away.

They paused when out of sight of the tribe, and before Latour knew well what had occurred, he was being tied to a tree.

"What means this ?" he yelled. "What have I done to you or yours ?"

"Nothing," Tinker Tom said, quietly ; "it is to prevent your doing harm that we do this."

They had bound him hands and feet to the massive trunk, and were going away when his frantic cries rang out with redoubled force.

"Hear me !" he shrieked. "Whatever may be the cause of this strange proceeding, believe me I shall not in any way interfere with you. I came as a friend, and would make a pro—— Curse them ! they are gone, and I am left powerless."

Monsieur Jules saw part of the pleasant fabric he had reared on the previous night tumble to pieces, and, struggling to free himself from his bonds, he invoked the direst curses upon the heads of his captors.

Curses or struggles availed him nothing in this dilemma. This he soon discovered, and his bloodshot eyes were turned wildly from point to point in the hope of beholding a peasant or one of the keepers from the Abbey.

When the child ran laughing at the success of her plan, she entered a small glade completely shut out by the surrounding trees. Here she was met by the fair, handsome boy who was lying at the old chief's feet when Tinker Tom brought the intelligence of Ralph's banishment from the tribe.

He sprang gladly forward when the beautiful child entered the secluded spot, and, gazing inquiringly at her flushed face, he asked—

"Have you been frightened that you came so quickly through the forest?"

"No, Jack, not frightened; I was running to escape that surly Latour. Papa told him to come with me, and I don't like him, so while he went back to fetch my basket I ran away." Here she became sad, and, dropping her voice, added—"But I must not stay; I only came to tell you that papa says I am never to speak to you again."

The colour came to the boy's face, and, throwing back his handsome head proudly, he said—

"The earl need not have told you this, Lily, for we go away to-day."

"Go away!" she repeated. "But you need not go, Jack; you told me you were not a gipsy, so—so, you can stay."

"I must go with them," he answered, bitterly, "though I do not like their mode of life; but I am not old enough yet to make my way through the world or else I—Hark! what is that?"

He caught the fair girl by the wrist, and as his face paled he bent down and listened intently.

"It seems like a man calling out for help," the boy said; then casting a startled look around, he added—"It is the man that came with you. Tinker Tom and Aiken have caught him."

Lily looked at the excited boy, and asked—

"What do they want with him, Jack?"

"I will tell you, Lily. They have been in the park all the morning watching for you; so run, Lily, run! Although they will beat me for not keeping you, I do not care."

The child became confused; she felt alarmed at her companion's words, but did not comprehend the danger he had but hinted at. The full significance soon came, and for some moments held her spellbound.

"They intend to take you away," he said, "forcibly, in revenge for the earl having transported Ralph. Don't cry, Lily; I will take you back to the Abbey, although," he added, "the gipsies tell me the earl is my greatest foe."

He grasped the fair small hand, and they ran silently from the little glade which had so oft rung with their happy laughter.

Jack Lennox knew that Tinker T—

would soon be upon their trail, and, determined, if possible, to save the child, he made a détour to reach the front of the Abbey, thinking by this means to escape the watchful gipsy.

The spire of the old gateway was visible between the trees, and keeping this in view, the fugitives ran swiftly onward. Another ten minutes and she would be safe; but ere half that brief space had passed, a quick footfall behind caused their hearts to sink.

"Stop!" a voice said—"stop! Do you hear, Jack Lennox? Stop! or I will put a charge of buck-shot in your back."

The boy came to a sudden halt, and, as he turned fiercely and faced his pursuer, he clasped his hands tightly, and seemed as though about to spring at Tinker Tom's throat.

"He will do it," said the boy. "I would not stop, Lily, had he not that gun with him."

Tinker Tom's face was purple with rage when he overtook the children, and, without a word, he seized the girl and threw her over his shoulder.

"Let her alone," said the boy, trying to interpose his small frame before the child. "I wish I had strength enough, you should not do this."

Tinker Tom's reply was a sudden blow with the gun-barrel. It struck Jack Lennox across the face, and hurled him bleeding to the earth.

The gipsy would have left the senseless boy but for the fear he would have gone to the Abbey and brought the keepers out to rescue the fair child.

He lifted the boy with as much ease as he would an infant, then, with his double burden, he started swiftly after the tribe.

Fearing the earl's anger when he discovered the loss of his little favourite, they had wisely made preparations to remove from the vicinity of the Abbey, and by the time Tinker Tom had recognized the girl they were far beyond the confines of the forest.

CHAPTER VI.

OUR HERO'S FIRST STEP IN THE WORLD.

EARL FALCONMERE'S horse fell soon after the fox was hunted from his cover. The leap had often been exceeded by the powerful hunter, but upon this occasion he was brought up too quickly, and instead of clearing a ditch that lay beyond the quickset hedge, his hind feet slid down the slippery incline, and the earl, to save himself, inadvertently jerked the animal's mouth and brought him over.

The horse and rider struggled for some time in the slimy filth, and had it not been for two labourers who were at work in an adjacent field, the last Earl of Falconmere would have terminated his existence in the foul stagnant water.

Though terribly shaken, the earl was able to remount, and rewarding the men, he turned the horse's head towards the Abbey and rode slowly away.

Covered with the mire from the ditch, the earl did not wish to pass the front of the Abbey. There was a near cut to the rear of the park by passing through the forest; this path the earl pursued, and to his amazement came upon his valet, bound hand and foot to the trunk of a tree.

To spring from his horse and loosen the bonds was the work of a moment, his heart throbbing violently, and his quivering lips refusing to ask the cause of Latour's strange predicament.

He had guessed the truth before Latour could speak, and when the valet told him that Lily had disappeared, he sprang into the saddle and galloped towards the Abbey.

Latour saw the noble beast clear the high fence at a bound, and hurrying as fast as his cramped limbs would permit, he reached the park just as the earl, at the head of a body of keepers, grooms, and stablemen, issued forth in search of the little Lily.

The earl carried a double-barrelled gun in his hands; both hammers were drawn back, and by the wild gleam in his dark eyes, Latour knew that his master would slay the abductors of his adopted child with as little remorse as he would bring down a partridge.

"Come with us, Latour," said the earl; "you can identify the ruffians who fastened you to the tree."

Thus commanded, Monsieur Jules had no alternative but to obey.

They reached the spot where the gipsies had encamped, and, save for the charred remains of a wood fire, there was no trace left to guide the pursuers.

The earl leant upon his gun, and looked around for a sign of the retiring gipsies. There was none; every footprint had been obliterated by several of the tribe drawing long green boughs after them.

This had effectually obliterated their footmarks upon the green sward, and though the men scanned every part within a hundred yards of the camping-ground, they were still at fault.

The earl bore the crushing blow without a murmur; his desire for revenge for the time was stronger than the effects of the sudden loss he had sustained.

There was still hope. The tribe could not have gone far, and the keepers, who had learnt a little woodcraft by so often tracking poachers when they stole from the preserves, now took the lead in the pursuit.

Spreading themselves out, they keenly examined every tree and shrub, and after an hour's torturing suspense, the earl's heart was gladdened by a shout from one of his men, which told that the tribe had been discovered.

A small remnant of an old discarded red cloak had been held by the sharp thorns of a wild briar. This discovery kept alive the faint hope that had nearly left the earl's heart when he found how well the tribe had hidden the path they had taken.

He sprang forward at the cry, and as the faint light grew stronger in his eyes, he gave the men stern and peremptory orders to shoot down the first of the gang if any resistance was offered.

An hour's search brought them within sight of the gipsies; the tribe were leisurely pursuing the open road when the shouts from the keepers attracted their attention.

They paid no heed to the loud commands for them to stop; not even one of the women turned her head to look from whence the cries came.

This indifference made the men yet more eager to overtake them, and dashing across a ploughed field, the earl and his party intercepted them.

They would have continued their march, had not the injunctive earl, his frame quivering with passion, called out in a voice of thunder—

"Halt! or, by Heaven! I will send the contents of this weapon among you."

They saw by the speaker's wild gestures, and the stern expression upon his pitiless face, that he would execute his threat unless they instantly complied.

At a signal from the grey-headed old chief, the gipsies became as though suddenly transformed to stone; then the venerable man, stepping to the front, asked in a calm voice the reason of this interference.

The earl made no reply, but pushing such of the gipsies that stood in his path aside, made his way to a small covered cart, and with savage violence tore the canvas away.

He had fully expected to have seen the sweet child beneath the rude covering, and when he found the cart contained little else save the cooking utensils and a few small articles of clothing, a terrible imprecation fell from his lips.

His ravings were those of a madman, and with a spring like an angry panther, he closed with the old chief, and gripped him by the throat.

"Where is she?" he yelled. "Speak, old man, or I will crush out your life! speak—tell me where you have hidden the child."

The young men of the tribe would have helped their chief, but awed by the superior numbers of the earl's party, they were compelled to stand and quietly behold the aged man nearly strangled in the earl's strong grasp.

"Take your fingers from my throat," the white-headed gipsy gasped. "I cannot answer you—I am choking. Would you commit murder?"

"Ay," was the fierce response as the earl relaxed his grip ; "I would dye this road with the blood of your accursed race for this foul crime. Tell me," he added with passionate energy, "where is the child you have stolen ?"

The old man pointed upwards, and raising his eyes solemnly towards heaven, answered :

"By the great Omnipotent I swear I have not seen a child this day, save the little ones of my tribe."

He looked like a patriarch of old as he stood thus, and even the fiery earl was for a moment struck with the simple grandeur of the humble gipsy.

Latour, who had scanned the faces of the men, bore out the chief's statement by coming to the earl's side and whispering—

"Neither of the fellows who tied me to the tree are here, my lord."

The earl's face grew paler at these words, and turning to the aged man, he asked—

"Are any of the tribe absent ? Speak truthfully—I am in no mood to be trifled with."

"The gipsy," said the chief, "has no need to lie. Two of the tribe are away ; they left us to join another party who are moving southward."

The earl groaned with anguish. He realized the fearful truth, and, clasping his burning brow with both hands, moaned—

"Lost, lost, lost !"

The folly of the men who had taken the child joining this party became apparent to the earl's followers, and the head gamekeeper, whose long services placed him upon a more familiar footing with the earl than his fellows, now advanced.

"It may not be too late, my lord," he said, respectfully. "We can, by going cross country, reach the London road almost as soon as the men who have taken Miss Lily ; that is," he added, "if they have gone in that direction."

The earl caught eagerly at the suggestion. "Is there no other road," he said, "except this and the high road to London ?"

"None other, my lord."

The keeper was left with half a dozen men to watch the gipsies, and rescue the child should her abductors join them.

This done, he turned from the road, and, forcing his way through the hedge-row, took the nearest path to the road that led to London.

When retracing the verge of the forest, the earl and his party were within twenty yards of the object of their search. They knew it not, and until night set in the pursuit was continued, then only abandoned when the men became worn out with fatigue.

The earl returned to the Abbey that night a crushed and broken-hearted man. He had lost all he loved upon earth, and cared not how soon the cold hand of death came upon him.

●　　●　　●　　●　　●

Tinker Tom carried the children through the forest, until the boy recovered his consciousness.

His first act was to struggle with the muscular gipsy, and with his puny fist to strike the fellow's dark, swarthy cheek.

Tinker Tom laughed at this show of spirit, and, placing him upon the ground, bade him follow and be silent.

The boy wiped the blood from his face, and, looking fiercely at the gipsy, said—

"I shall be a man some day, then I will make you sorry for taking her away."

The burly gipsy was both pleased and amused at the lad's latent spirit, and, placing Lily on the ground, said—

"There, my young game-cock, take the little lady's hand, and follow me. No noise, mind, if we should meet any one in the forest, or I will give you another taste of this." He touched the gun-barrel significantly as he spoke. "And as for the girl, I will twist her neck."

Tinker Tom had the repute of being what is termed a man of his word. Jack Lennox had upon more than one occasion seen him carry out a threat to the very letter, and fearing that he would strangle the fair girl, he promised not to call out for help, no matter whom they might meet.

Tinker Tom knew the boy would not break faith with him. Though so young, he showed the better clay from which he was moulded, by a strict adherence to the truth, and an absence of the pilfering proclivities so common with the juvenile members of the vagabond tribe.

This matter settled, the gipsy threw his gun into the hollow of his left arm, and bidding the children go in advance, the walk through the forest was resumed.

The little girl felt less fear now the man had placed her upon the ground, and her hand was clasped in that of her young play-fellow ; she clung to him, and showed more calmness than could have been expected from one placed in such a strange position.

They had not got far when the earl's stately figure was visible through the trees, and had not Jack reminded her of Tinker

Tom's threat, she would have called out to him for help.

The gipsy made them creep behind a clump of bushes until the earl had passed, then he arose and urged them quickly forward.

When they neared the road, which was at that moment being traversed by the tribe, the earl and his party could be seen approaching. Again the children were forced into a place of concealment. Here they remained until the pursuers were seen returning from their unsuccessful visit to the tribe.

The trunk of an old tree hid their forms from the earl and his men, and as Lily stood clinging to her young companion, she whispered—

"Let us run when papa and his men come close."

Tinker Tom stood some yards in front of them, both hands grasping his gun, and his dark face full of triumph as he watched the keepers breaking through the thick vegetation.

He heard Lily's whispering, and as he glanced at the advancing party, he said, savagely—

"Make the attempt, and I will kill you both."

Lily shrank back, and clung yet closer to her companion; and he, as though to shield her from harm, passed one arm round her waist, and clasped her hand.

Anger and despair were blended in the look he gave Tinker Tom; then turning his head towards Lily, he whispered—

"Never mind; I will try and take you to the Abbey to-night."

She felt he would keep his word, and when the earl again passed within twenty yards of the place of their concealment, she remained perfectly quiet.

Tinker Tom laughed mockingly when the men were out of hearing, and again driving the children before him, he went after his companions.

They had just crept through a hedge when the gipsy, with a lowly-muttered oath, dragged the young girl back, and forcing her down, crouched beside her in the shelter of a dry ditch.

Jack Lennox he had already disposed of by hurling him to the ground. The boy looked up in surprise at this sudden attack, and was about to ask the reason, when Tinker Tom placed the forefinger of his right hand upon his lips, and with his left pointed towards a group of men who were partially hidden by the trees.

Jack knew the men at the first glance; some he recognised as gamekeepers, others by their livery were grooms in the service of Earl Falconmere.

These men were the party left by the head keeper to watch the road by which the gipsy tribe were travelling.

Until nightfall, Tinker Tom and his young companions remained in their place of concealment. The watchers at times passing so close that their words were plainly distinguishable.

The boy's heart beat painfully when he heard the men. He knew that one cry would bring them to Lily's rescue, and several times the effort to repress the words that came to his lips was noticed by Tinker Tom.

He brought the muzzle of his gun in line with the boy's head, and in a voice like the hiss of a snake, said—

"Remember, the slightest cry, and I will pull the trigger."

Jack Lennox cowered before the savage expression in the gipsy's eyes, and bowing his head, wept at the misfortune that had befallen the little girl—a misfortune, in spite of the strong wish within, he was powerless to avert.

He saw Lily's tearful blue eyes regarding him with an expression of mute entreaty, and construing that glance as it was intended, he remained silent; but his brain was busy with a plan by which he yet hoped to effect her deliverance.

There was not a selfish thought in this. He hoped only to take the trembling child to the gates of the old Abbey; then he would return and meet the punishment he felt assured would befall him. For this he cared not. Too oft had he been lashed by the gipsies for refusing to aid them in their petty thefts, to shrink when the liberty, perhaps the life, of the fair child was at stake.

"I'll do it," he thought; "and they may tie me to the cart-wheel, if they like; even then I shall not care, if Lily is safe."

The punishment he alluded to would have caused a stout heart to quail at the very thought. He had seen, and his flesh had quivered at the sight, strong men stripped to the waist and bound hand and foot to the cart-wheel, then lashed with a whip, the thongs of which were composed of thin strips of cowhide. He had seen the flesh torn and lacerated by this inhuman punishment; yet he could bear it to save the little girl from the power of the vagrant tribe.

When the bright stars shone from heaven's vaulted canopy, Tinker Tom left his hiding-place. The men who had been left by the earl's order had gone towards the Abbey, tired of watching, and hopeful that the child they all loved would be recovered before their return.

The gipsy, holding the children on either side of him, started swiftly in the track of his tribe. The walk was long and arduous, for he kept inside the hedgerow, and before they reached the camp, Lily's feet were torn and blistered by the rugged ground.

They had travelled ploughed fields, the earth dried by the sun and wind until each piece was as hard to walk over as jagged stones. Oft, too, had the child become ankle-deep in mud, as her captor stumbled into a ditch. So, with aching limbs, aching heart, and the large tears falling silently upon her soft cheek, she was dragged to the presence of the vengeful gipsies.

The women of the tribe would have soothed her, but she shrank from them and clung to the boy, and with her head nestled to his breast, sobbed with agony.

He drew her away from the dark circle of these rude beings whose very presence filled the child with alarm, and as he bent over her, and smoothed the long sunny tresses which fell like a golden shower upon her neck, he whispered words of hope.

"Do not sleep to-night, Lily," he said, "and I will try and take you from these people. There is a withered tree near the road-side. Wait until everything is quiet in the camp, then go to that tree; I shall be there, and we will go back to the Abbey."

She did not answer, her heart was too full. Then Jack, taking her by the hand, led her to the fire, and gave her a portion of the savoury stew from the huge iron pot.

"Eat," he whispered; "it will make you strong enough to undergo the long journey to-night."

He saw the child's weary look, and his heart misgave him. He knew they would have to be fleet of foot to escape, and with the hope that her strength would return when she had partaken of the nourishing viands, he pressed her to eat that from which her delicate palate revolted.

The signal was given for the gipsies to retire, and Lily was led by one of the women to the shelter of the canvas tilt, which by day covered the cart and at night served for a tent.

Jack Lennox lay near Tinker Tom, and as the night wore on, he heard the gipsy's heavy respiration increase as his senses became steeped in slumber.

The boy raised himself on his elbow and listened intently. Everything was quiet in the camp; even the restless watch-dogs — the gipsies' vigilant and trusty sentinels — were coiled up within reach of the warmth which came from the dusky fire-glow.

As noiseless as ever an Indian scout moved within the circle of an enemy's wigwams, the boy quitted his companion's side, and crept towards the cart.

It was but the work of a moment to draw Tinker Tom's gun from among the loose straw; then with a swift and noiseless tread he ran towards the withered tree.

Eager and anxious was the search he made around the gnarled old trunk, and when he satisfied himself that the fair girl had not yet left the camp, he leant upon the fowling-piece and strained his eyes towards the dim outline of the gipsies' tents.

Half an hour passed—to him it was a lifetime—and then the brave little heart began to sink with apprehension.

"She will not come," he said, in low, sad tones. "What shall I do? Has she been detected in her attempt to escape, or has the exertion she has gone through this day caused her to sleep?"

He heard the sweet chime from a distant village proclaim the hour. To him the sound came like a knell; the child could not come to him, and all hope of seeing her would pass away.

So ran his thoughts. The morn was fast approaching, and daylight, he felt, would be his greatest foe.

He trembled with excitement as these thoughts passed through his mind, and in another instant he would have returned to the camp, and sought the fair child in spite of every risk.

His first step was arrested by the sound of a heavy footfall hastily approaching the place where he stood.

Well versed in the cunning mode by which the gipsies eluded the gamekeepers' search, the boy laid himself face downward, and with a noiseless, snake-like motion glided towards the dark hedgerow.

He had safely hidden himself beneath the overhanging bushes by the time the solitary wayfarer reached the tree.

There was sufficient light to discern the man's features, and Jack Lennox, as he recognized in the man one of the tribe, gave a start of surprise.

The gipsy had gone forth the preceding morn in company with Tinker Tom, and as the startled boy saw him pause and look back at short intervals, he began to fear that the absence of this man boded ill to Falcon-mere's proud earl.

He had heard the threats of revenge when the gipsies met in council, and as he saw Tinker Tom's companion going swiftly towards the camp, a chill came over his young frame.

"If he awakes Tinker Tom," thought the boy, "I shall be discovered; then"—he paused for a moment, then jumping to his feet added—"then I will use this gun before they shall do any harm to the poor little girl."

The deep bay of a watch-dog came upon his ears, then the angry voice of the gipsy as he reproached the hound for not recognizing his footsteps.

With bated breath Jack Lennox listened to these sounds, and the ruddy hue of health faded from his cheeks, and left them as pallid as those of the sheeted dead.

Every sense was concentrated as he placed his ear to the ground, and his heart throbbed quickly, as he feared the savage tones of Tinker Tom's voice would follow the noises already detailed.

"I had better return," soliloquized the boy, sorrowfully. "Lily will not come now, and should I be missed, that brute will come in search. Ha! she is here."

He ran eagerly forward as the fair-haired child advanced towards him. She had come, but in a different direction to that which he expected.

"I have been so frightened," she said, as she placed her hand confidingly in his. "I saw you take something from beneath the cart, and would have come from the tent but I was afraid."

"Afraid, Lily?—of the woman?"

"Yes; she said such dreadful things to me that I have cried ever since, and the time seemed so long. Every time that the hour struck from the church I felt worse; but when two o'clock came I thought of you, and how sorry you would be, so I crept out and walked a long way round away from where the men are sleeping, to come here. I was afraid of the dogs."

They were walking hand in hand upon the smooth footway as the child told her young champion how heavily the time had passed since she had been taken to the tent.

"I am glad you are here," he said, "but we must make haste, for fear they may discover your escape. Can you run, Lily?"

"I could, but my feet are sore; but," she added, cheerfully, "I will try."

They began at a gentle pace, and the warmth stilling the pains of her blistered feet, their speed increased, and was continued until both were panting with exertion.

This run had placed a couple of hundred yards between them and the camp, and for the first time since he had stolen from Tinker Tom's side, Jack Lennox began to breathe freely.

He began to impart the joyful feeling of security to his companion, but she suddenly stopped his speech by abruptly asking—

"What have you brought that gun with you for?"

"I took it away," Jack said, "to prevent Tinker Tom from shooting us, should he come. Lily—Lily! here—hide quick—here he is."

The words came from trembling lips and as the young fugitives sought the shelter of the hedge, they heard a man's hasty steps coming towards them.

They needed no light to distinguish his form, for the dreaded voice of Tinker Tom could be heard calling upon Jack Lennox to stop.

The boy dropped upon one knee, and as a fierce light came to his eyes and a terrible resolution nerved his arms, he raised the butt of the fowling-piece to his shoulder, and in reply to the fair child's exclamation of alarm, answered—

"If he attempts to take you back, Lily, I will shoot him."

She cowered beside the handsome, resolute boy, her terror holding her speechless and spellbound.

Tinker Tom had been awakened by the man who had passed so closely where our hero crouched. He had missed the boy, and the truth at once came to his mind.

With a frightful oath he sprang to his feet and ran to the tent where Lily had been taken. She had gone; and the gipsy telling his companion to take the fields, he bounded to the road, and soon saw the dim outlines of the children's forms as they ran onward.

He saw them turn from the footway and disappear, and running hastily towards the hedge, beheld the boy's attitude of defence.

Tinker Tom was unarmed, and he knew sufficient of Jack Lennox's determination to cause him to pause ere he sought to recapture the little maiden.

"Put down that gun," he said, hoarsely, "and return to the camp, or I will have you flogged as the tribe flogs those who steal from each other."

The boy's firmly spoken reply staggered the angry gipsy, and overawed him in spite of his brute courage and immense muscular power.

"I shall do neither," he said, "and as sure as the stars are above us I will shoot you if you attempt to take the little girl from my side."

The muzzle of the fowling-piece was in line with the gipsy's head, and the finger that coiled around the trigger, though small, was but waiting for a hostile movement to send forth the heavy charge of buckshot with which the piece was loaded.

Tinker Tom stood silent with rage and astonishment, and grinding his teeth with passion, he listened intently for the sound of his companion's footsteps.

"If he can get behind the young cub," Tinker Tom thought, "I can easily retake the girl."

The man he so anxiously listened for must have wandered far away from the narrow rath which ran parallel with the hedge, for some minutes passed and no sign or sound denoted his whereabouts.

Goaded to madness at the thought of the child's escape, Tinker Tom made a sudden bound forward to snatch the gun from the brave little fellow.

He came within a foot of the dangerous muzzle, then a sharp report broke the stillness, and Tinker Tom fell to the ground, his leg shattered by the close discharge.

Jack Lennox waited but to see that his foe had fallen, then throwing the gun away, he seized Lily's hand, and started forward at a pace that fear alone could have caused.

The ground was now familiar to the young fugitives; they were rapidly nearing the grand old park that stood in the rear of the Abbey. Joy! before another twenty minutes would expire, Lily would be safe.

They entered the earl's domain by passing through the broken fence. Here every tree was familiar to the young pair; here the boy had often entered to join the fair and beautiful girl in her childish sport.

He thought of this as she endeavoured to keep pace with him, an effort which gave her the most exquisite pain, for her limbs were weary, and but for the danger that yet menaced her, she would gladly have sought a brief respite by lying upon the cold, damp earth.

"We are safe," he began—"safe, and I will now leave. See! What is that?"

Four streaks of livid light lit up the Abbey's sombre walls as this exclamation left his lips. Higher and higher rose the red light, and the points, like serpents' tongues, licked and crawled round the four high towers which formed the angles of Falconmere Abbey.

The children paused, awe-struck by the fearful sight, and as the windows reflected back the red light, the fair girl clung to her companion's arm and moaned piteously—

"The Abbey is on fire! Poor papa, poor papa; he will be burnt!"

Lily's words roused Jack from the momentary stupefaction that had fallen upon him, and dragging her quickly forward, he exclaimed—

"It is their work! Quick, Lily; we shall yet be in time to give the alarm!"

The wind fanned the flame until it spread like a winding sheet around the doomed walls.

Showers of sparks began to start upward, and the roar of the terrible element could be plainly heard by the terrified children.

Their pathway was as light as if the noonday sun shone among the trees, and yielding to the excitement caused by the grand yet sad sight, they flew onward—pain, weariness and danger alike forgotten.

The sudden pealing of the great bell was now heard even above the roaring flames, then came a confused and heart-rending succession of shrieks as the female domestics rushed wildly from the blazing pile.

The hurrying forms of men flitted like shadows before the children, and amid the wild scene of chaotic terror and confusion they reached the lawn in front of the Abbey.

The young girl's return was unsuspected in such a scene, and many who now rushed wildly to and fro, and passed the pale, lovely child, were among those who sought so eagerly but a few hours before to snatch her from the power of the wandering vagrants.

Latour, carrying a leathern valise upon his shoulder, passed within a few paces of the boy who he hoped would finish the erection of the glowing fabric he had so well outlined.

He saw them not. The all-absorbing thought of saving himself and the precious contents of the valise from the fierce element, drove every other subject from his mind.

Every moment added to the remorseless power of the fell destroyer. One of the mighty walls had fallen in, and men who were risking life and limb to stay the advance of the insidious foe, shrank back terror-stricken, at the terrible crash of the falling masonry.

There was yet another sight in the night's dread work—a sight that caused strong men to turn pale, and their hearts to stand still.

There came a cry from those who directed the stream of water upon the front of the building—a cry that was taken up until it swelled into a chorus of affrighted voices; and the fair girl who clung to her boyish companion, hearing the dread sounds, gave a piercing scream, and fell to the earth.

Jack Lennox drew the senseless child away from the rushing feet of the excited men as they ran beneath the earl's chamber, and a hundred voices took up the dreadful words which had stricken the fair girl to the earth.

"Save the earl! Save the earl!"

Such were the words which betokened the nobleman's danger, and every eye turning towards the open casement, around which the hungry flames played, beheld the peer grasping the window-sill, and frantically calling upon those below to save him.

Men who had grown grey in the peer's service, and whose devotion to their master made them reckless of their own danger, reared a ladder amid the fire, and as they were beaten back, scorched and half suffocated, the flames caught the ladder and consumed the lower part before the earl could even risk this fearful mode of escape.

A mighty cry came from the strong men's

lips when they saw the charred fragments fall amid the hissing fire. That cry was echoed by one from the earl as the flames drove him back from the window; then came a fearful crash, a column of smoke and fiery sparks shot upward, and the front of the palatial mansion fell to the ground.

Jack Lennox had watched this fearful scene with distended eyes and bated breath, and when all hope of saving the earl had passed away, he turned sadly towards the recumbent form by his side, and the utter loneliness of their position broke upon him.

What could he do? He had not a friend in the world save the gipsies, and after what had passed between them he felt it would be madness to return.

He saw Lily's blue eyes unveiled, and heard her lowly-spoken words as she asked for her papa. The boy felt thankful that she had been spared the sight of the earl's destruction. A soothing reply was upon his lips, but ere it could find utterance, he caught Lily's hand convulsively and drew her further in the shade.

A gesture to imply silence answered her interrogative look; and, taking his finger from his lips, he pointed towards two figures which were crouching behind a tall tree.

The girl's face became pale, and her large eyes dilated with fear as she recognized the hateful forms of two of the tribe.

The children could hear their lowly-spoken converse, and mixed with the exultant expressions at the fate which had befallen the Abbey, were words of dread import to herself and her young protector.

"Lily," whispered the boy, "we must go away from here. You hear what they mean to do if we are caught."

She clasped his hand, and, half stupified with grief at her sudden bereavement, suffered him to lead her from the scene of her great sorrow.

Once only they paused, and Lily looked sadly back at the smoking ruins of her childhood's happy home. She sobbed bitterly when she thought of the kindly man who had been her all upon earth. Then turning away, as she remembered her cruel persecutors were but a little distance from them, she looked in her young companion's face, and asked—

"Where are we going?"

"I know not," the boy answered; "anywhere to escape the tribe. London, I think, Lily, will be the best place. We are now *out on the world*, and without a home or a friend."

The child had no knowledge of the meaning attached to these words. She knew not they meant hunger, thirst, and not a place to hide their heads from the cold damps of evening, or a shilling to purchase food. The poor little wayfarers were indeed OUT ON THE WORLD.

CHAPTER VII.

A ROAD-SIDE ACQUAINTANCE.

THE brave little fellow's heart was sorely tried by that long and wretched journey to the great metropolis. Eight days and nights were passed ere the ragged, wayworn pair beheld the dim outlines of the great city looming out, sombre and massive, in the twilight.

Eight days! What misery and despair had been compressed in that brief space! What strange scenes they had passed through, and how oft, in after years, they recalled the harsh rebuke they had met from those whom they had sought to relieve their dire distress!

Walking onward by day, and begging a morsel of bread at the open doors of the humble cotters; at night sleeping in a barn or beneath a haystack—save once, when a kindly woman gave them a shelter with her little ones.

She had little else to give the hungry children, for the scanty morning meal was not sufficient to satisfy the cravings of four flaxen-haired youngsters whom she had to support; but she could not see them go upon their pilgrimage without food, so a small portion was eked out, and they left the poor widow's humble cot with lighter hearts than had fallen to their lot during the five days that had elapsed since Falconmere's proud walls fell to the earth.

The sixth day was, perhaps, the worst time they had experienced. Twice Jack had sought charity. Each time he had been refused, and threatened, in the second instance, with a horsewhip if he did not leave the village.

The latent fire in the boy's nature blazed in his angry eyes at the brutal threat, and as he turned away to rejoin his companion, the small hands were clenched, and his eyes filled with tears at his inability to chastise the untaught peasant.

This fierceness left him when he looked upon Lily's pale, pinched face, and as she ran forward with outstretched hands to receive the scanty morsel she expected, Jack burst out into an angry flood of tears, and said, savagely—

"I have nothing, Lily; the—the——"

His passion would not permit him to finish the sentence for some moments, then he stamped his foot upon the ground, and resumed—

"I don't care for myself; it's you, Lily. I can go without until we get to London."

He had a vague idea that in the "million-peopled city" every want would be supplied.

"Never mind, Jack," the child said, placing her hand upon his shoulder; "I am not hungry. See—I have found this while waiting for you, and eaten part."

She held a raw turnip towards the boy. It had fallen from a pail of offal which a man was carrying to the piggery. He had kicked it into the road, and from thence it was taken by the hungry child—fit food for one who had been so delicately nurtured!

Jack Lennox was hungry. Fain would he have shared the prize; but even in this, as in all things else, he would not eat until the fair child had partaken of two-thirds of this wretched apology for a breakfast.

A refreshing draught from a small running stream finished their repast; then the journey was resumed.

With eager eyes they read the milestones as they passed, and each told that they were slowly decreasing the distance between them and the great city.

Ten miles the children journied that day, and when footsore and worn out, they were compelled to seat themselves upon a heap of stones by the roadside.

"XXI. MILES TO LONDON."

They were opposite the stone which bore this inscription, and Jack, looking in the direction pointed out by a ghostly fingerpost, repeated the inscription several times.

"Twenty-one miles, Lily," he said, at length. "We have come nearly sixty. This won't seem much, will it?"

Lily raised her eyes; she had been watching a number of ants, and thinking how much better off the little creatures were than herself.

"They have a place to sleep in," she thought, "and plenty to eat; I have neither."

She was wondering when the present wretchedness would terminate, when Jack's voice aroused her.

"I am glad we have not to go far," she said, "for I could not walk much more, Jack; but," she added, suddenly, "what are we to do when we get to London?"

The abrupt question somewhat startled our hero, and as he had not the least idea of his course of action, he remained silent. He had heard wondrous stories of fortunate lads entering the smoky place with a fourpenny-piece in their pocket and becoming rich men, but how this was accomplished he had not the least idea. So, while puzzling his brain how he should answer Lily's query, the words were repeated.

"I don't quite know yet, Lily," he said, rising. "Come, let us walk a little farther, to those houses in the hollow, and while we are walking, I'll perhaps think of something."

The cluster of small dwellings indicated by Jack was situated about half a mile from the place where they had been sitting.

They travelled about half this distance in silence, for the boy had not yet resolved upon any plan that seemed likely to better their condition.

Lily was silent, and her little lips were tightly compressed. She was suffering the most excruciating pain from the blisters which covered her feet; she felt weak and ill for the want of nourishment as well, and though every step sent a thrill through her frame, and she felt that it would be a priceless boon to lie quietly by the road-side, she uttered no word of complaint.

She knew how ardently the boy wished to reach the great city of the world, and as a reward for the trials and privations he underwent upon her account, she would have fallen upon the footway before a word or any indication of her sufferings came from her lips.

Both had their eyes cast down, when a light footfall caused them to look up, and, within twenty yards of them they beheld a boy, apparently a few years older than our hero.

He was coming towards them, and by his glance as he passed he was evidently as much surprised to meet the young wayfarers as they were to meet him.

There was ample time for the children to examine the stranger before he passed, and they saw that as far as outward appearance went, he was much on a par with themselves.

His clothes were stained and very dusty, and from the fact of their not having been made for him, they looked infinitely worse than they really were.

The jacket would have buttoned comfortably round the chest of a youth twice the new comer's size, and the superfluous cloth in this article might have been added with advantage to the bottoms of his trousers.

He had a greater length of limb than our hero, but he wanted that lithe movement and well-knit frame which Jack Lennox possessed.

His feet were large, so were his hands, but his frame seemed small for his height; and that which struck Jack, as he took a sidelong glance at the stranger, was the "old look" upon his features. He was not ill-looking, but a shrewd, half-cunning expression, which seemed to have grown upon him, made the face appear older by many years than it really was.

When they had passed each other Jack involuntarily turned his head, and found the stranger was looking back also. A half-smile lit up the latter's face, and evidently looking upon this as a wish for our hero to speak, he turned back, and was soon beside the young pair.

"You seem tired," he said, in an easy, familiar manner. "Have you tramped far to-day?"

Jack did not know whether to resist this overture, or to make a further acquaintance with the young gentleman who possessed such a plenitude of jacket.

A moment's reflection caused him to do the latter. The stranger had come from the village, and perhaps would take Lily to a cottage where she could receive both food and rest. This thought shaped his answer.

"Yes," he said, "we have come a long way."

"So have I," the communicative youth said, "and no luck. Have you had any?"

The vision of the cottage faded from Jack's mind. The stranger, after all, did not belong to the village. Our hero felt sorry he had encouraged the stranger's advance, and was meditating whether he should give him to understand that his company was not required, when Lily struck her foot against a loose stone, and gave a scream of agony.

This caused Jack to lead the fair girl to a similar resting-place to that which they had before used, and ere she had sufficiently recovered to resume the journey, the two boys were as familiar as though they had known each other from infancy.

The stranger made Jack acquainted with the causes which led to this meeting without the least reserve, and our hero saw that, so far from discouraging the acquaintance, it would be well to court it by offering him a share in their Joint-Stock Company of Misery (Unlimited).

An offer which was received with evident pleasure. But, stay. I must first inform my readers of the causes which led to this arrangement.

The trio had not sat long upon the small pyramid of stones, when Jack asked his free-and-easy companion about the small village which lay in the tranquil-looking valley.

"Yes, I have been there," the stranger answered. "Not much to be made there, but——"

"We are not common beggars," Jack said, proudly. He was not quite reconciled to the gentleman's peculiar manners then. "It was not to learn how much or little was to be obtained——"

The stranger laughed, and placed his hand patronizingly upon Jack's shoulder, as he said—

"No offence—no offence, I hope. Common beggars! No, certainly not. But, come, now; speak the truth. You are—eh, you understand?"

Jack did not understand, nor did he like the facetious dig in the ribs which accompanied the words.

Jack made a fierce answer, and clenched his hands; but the stranger, so far from taking umbrage at this show of spirit, only laughed the louder, and made a quiet remark which totally put our hero's dignity and anger to flight.

He could not, for the life of him, forbear laughing, and Lily, in spite of her pain, joined in the merriment.

This opened the way to a better understanding, and Jack freely expressed the state of his affairs.

The stranger looked much concerned when he heard of the scanty meal they had shared before starting upon the day's weary travel.

A desultory conversation ensued after this. Then the topic changed to their meeting.

"I like you both," the stranger said, frankly, when this subject was broached, "and as you will require a guide when you get to London, I see no reason why I should not fulfil that important post. Suppose I tell you a little about myself as we walk to the village?"

The stranger skilfully out-flanked our hero, and placing himself between him and the young girl, began before Jack could alter this arrangement.

"A few words," he said, "will do, but as we have some distance to go, I will make it as long as possible. To begin, I never had the felicity of knowing my parents, if I ever had any. I was found, I believe, by a policeman, wrapped up in brown paper."

Jack and Lily both laughed outright.

"What are you laughing at?" asked the strange youth.

"The policeman," Jack answered. "You said he was wrapped up in brown paper."

"I meant myself," said the stranger, "not the policeman. Well, he took me to the workhouse until I was claimed, but as that event never came off, they kept me until I was fourteen; then I was apprenticed to a tailor, but as my master was fond of trying the strength of his sleeve-board upon my skull, we parted about a fortnight since, and I started to seek my fortune—a search, by the way, which has been very unproductive at present.

"My name? Oh, I had forgotten that. Robert Jawkins was the aristocratic one given me by the board. The sleeve-board? Bless you, no; by the workhouse board. Do I mean a board? Decidedly; but the workhouse board was composed of a number of wooden-headed men, and the other——Eh? Why did they give me that name? I believe it was in consequence of the initials R. J. being found upon my brown paper suit, but somehow this name was only used by the

MONSIEUR JULES LATOUR MEETS WITH A MISHAP.

workhouse people. Everybody else came to the conclusion that my rightful name was Long Bob, for by this I have been known since my farewell adieu to the people who gave me over to the gin-drinking little tailor.

"Do I know much of London? Well, yes; a trifle. My master, when he was not engaged in the attempt to split his sleeve-board upon my cranium, was in the habit of standing in front of a gin-shop bar, and I, relieved for a time from the operation, found it more congenial to mix with the boys who were wont to congregate at the corner of the street. They were at first rather free with their remarks. At one time I was honoured by being called 'Work'us;' at others, 'Cabbage,' 'Snip,' and so on; but a few fights having set matters straight and several noses bleeding, they found out also that my proper name was Long Bob, and I found out from them much information about the great place called London; for though I had been left as a legacy to the old city, in consequence of the very strict rules of the boarding-school I was reared at, I knew as little about the place as you do. I will tell you about that another time. We are close to the village, and if your history is very long I shall not hear it to-night."

After this direct hint Jack could not refuse imparting his history to Long Bob, and before they entered the single straggling street, the runaway apprentice was in possession of both Jack and Lily's history.

Long Bob seized our hero's hands when he had finished his simple narrative.

"Well done!" he said, admiringly; "you have acted bravely in shooting down that rascally gipsy."

He passed many flattering encomiums upon the little lady's courage in undertaking the long journey, and wound up by the assurance that he would stick to them until the party who wrapped his infantile form in brown paper offered a thousand pounds reward for any information that would lead to his recovery.

"As this will never occur," he said, "I do not think we shall part company very soon."

Jack said he hoped not, and Lily echoed this sentiment. The young pair looked upon the alliance with Robert Jawkins as a most fortunate circumstance. They saw, in spite of his quaint manner and peculiar mode of speech, that he possessed a keen perceptive power; this, added to his knowledge of the Great City, gave them brighter hopes of the hidden future.

When they reached the village, the hungry children stopped abruptly in front of a little shop devoted to the sale of such homely edibles as the inhabitants required.

There was a pyramid of fresh, crisp-looking loaves in one corner of the window; next to this tempting display was a dish of boiled bacon fresh from the saucepan. To the starving pair this sight had a strange fascination, and they stood wistfully regarding it with their pale, pinched faces close to the glass.

Long Bob saw the true state of affairs at a glance, and, turning over a solitary two-shilling piece in his pocket, he muttered, "Poor little things, they are indeed hungry; two shillings —now how can I lay it out to the best advantage? A loaf will be threepence ha'penny. What's that bacon a pound?— About tenpence I should think. Suppose I say half a pound of that. Three and a half and five makes eight and a half, then I shall have one, three and a half left. The shilling will get the poor little girl a bed; Jack and I will sleep in the fields——"

"I wish," Lily said, plaintively, and the low, painful words abruptly stopped R. J.'s meditations, "we had a piece of that bread. Do you think the woman would give me a piece if I ask?"

There was a suspicious moisture in Long Bob's eyes as he blustered out—

"I'll go and see—you stand here."

Two strides brought him to the counter, and face to face with a red-faced portly dame, the owner of the general store.

She had been watching the little hungry-looking faces since the sight of her viands brought the children to a standstill, and when Long Bob entered, as she supposed to beg, her ruddy face became ruddier, and, extending her large red hand towards the door, she said—

"That is the way out, young man. We never encourages vagrants in the village, so be off!"

This reception somewhat staggered R. J., but he was soon himself again, and, looking contemptuously at the dame, he placed his solitary coin upon the counter, and said—

"Your speech, my rustic Venus, does your good nature credit; but as I have no time to tell you a little wholesome truth, no words need pass between us. I'll take a loaf and half a pound of bacon—here's the coin."

The good lady whipped the money from under Long Bob's fingers, and, after biting it between her teeth, gave him the articles he desired.

There was not another shop in the village, or Long Bob would not have tamely put up with this. He thought of the little ones outside, and restrained his indignation until he had possession of the food and the change of his two-shilling piece; then, looking solemnly at the woman, he said—

"Yes, it must be so; my mother never yet foretold a death but it always happened.

Poor, miserable woman ! last night, when the gipsies read the stars, one fell upon the roof of this very place ; it foretold your death."

He turned abruptly and left the shop, to prevent the woman seeing the difficulty he had to keep his risible muscles under control.

He had good cause for laughter, for the dame's ruddy face became as white as though she had already succumbed to the grim destroyer, and, when he peered through the window, he saw her clutching at a small coffee-mill which was fixed at the corner of a row of shelves.

"She won't get over that to-night," thought Long Bob ; "the superstitious old fool !" Then aloud, as he rejoined the children, "Here, Jack, divide this with your little sweetheart."

How eagerly the poor boy clutched at and tore the loaf asunder ! and though his heart was full of gratitude for Long Bob's kindness, he could not utter a word of thanks until he had placed by far the largest portion in Lily's hands.

He forgot, also, to ask their companion to share the food with them ; had he done so, R. J. would have refused, although he had not eaten since early that morn.

He saw the wolfish, ravenous manner in which the children tore the loaf piecemeal, and, turning his head away from the painful sight, tried to whistle the air of a popular song to keep down the choking, hysterical feeling that came in his throat.

Poor fellow ! he had seen men and women suffering from hunger, but a sight like this was too much for him.

By the time they had finished the needful nourishment, Long Bob had managed to swallow the unpleasant sensation that came to his throat; he had also succeeded in getting up a very respectable attempt at finishing the tune, which attempt signally failed at the commencement.

"Feel better now ?" he asked. "Come on, we will look out for a place for Lily to sleep."

"Much better," Jack said ; "how kind of you to buy us——"

"Fal de dal ral. I say, Jack, we shall be near London this time to-morrow. I wonder how old Snip gets on with his sleeve-board practice ?"

The fair girl placed her small, wasted hand upon Long Bob's wrist, and said—

"You were indeed kind, and we never even asked you to have——"

"Couldn't touch a morsel," said Bob, interrupting her ; "I had dinner with Duke Humphrey to-day."

The children looked in his face, and opened their eyes with astonishment.

"Had dinner with a duke?" Jack said ; "a real duke ?"

Long Bob flourished his hand, and said—

"Duke Humphrey. Bless you, have you never heard of Duke Humphrey ?"

"Never," they both said in a breath.

"Well, to think of that !" said Long Bob. "Why, hundreds of people have dined with him every day—breakfast and tea, as well, sometimes."

"He must be very rich," said Jack, simply.

"Well, yes ; but, you see, the dinners do not cost him anything. Here we are. This is the only public-house here. You two sit down while I go inside."

"It strikes me," Bob thought, as he went to the bar, "we shall have to dine with the duke to-morrow unless something turns up."

By the time he had arrived at this conclusion he reached the bar. There was no one present save the hostess, and Bob's perception of character having been considerably sharpened by his early training, he saw at a glance that the bustling landlady was of a more genial, kindly temperament than the proprietress of the grocery store.

With a frankness that won the good lady's heart Bob stated the object of his visit.

"I have," he said, "a shilling and a few coppers ; the shilling I will pay for the little girl's bed, and what is left for her breakfast ; that is," he added, "if it can be done at the price."

There was a half-smile upon the good woman's face as she listened to Bob's offer, and before she gave him an answer, she asked where the two boys intended to pass the night.

"We don't much care," he said ; "it isn't very cold yet, except just before daylight, so a roost in a barn or under a haystack will do for us."

Lily and Jack were sent for, and the landlady heard from the little girl's lips the strange story in detail, and when Lily told how they had suffered since they started upon the weary journey, the good dame's cheeks were wet with tears.

"I am able," she said, "to befriend you to-night, but you must all leave early in the morning, as my husband does not like strange children in the house."

She did not tell the child that for this charitable deed she would, if known to her husband, be beaten worse than a dog, by the man who had sworn at the altar to love and cherish her through life.

Happily for the children the brute had gone to a market town a considerable distance from the village, and would not return until the following morning.

That night the children were regaled to repletion, and the hostess, who had taken a strange liking to Lily, gave the child a share of her bed.

Long Bob and Jack Lennox were shown to a small, comfortable chamber, and left to the undisturbed enjoyment of a cosy bed.

"Much better than the haystack," remarked Bob, as he drew the clean bed covering over his chin. "Good-hearted woman—eh, Jack?"

"Yes, she is. How kind to take poor little Lily to her bed room."

"She's a trump, Jack, and no mistake; and if ever I am claimed by a great man—it may happen, you know. Just fancy some fine morning a thousand hand-bills posted all over London, headed, "Proclamation!" then the Duke of Yorkshire offering a large reward for the infant that was wrapped in a sheet of brown paper marked with the letters R. J. What are you grinning for? it might happen. If it does, I will make this good woman a rich present for her kindness. She deserves it—eh, Jack?"

Jack Lennox replied in a sleepy tone—

"Yes."

"Don't go to sleep, old fellow. I want to talk to you."

"I must sit up, then," said the tired boy, "for I cannot keep my eyes open."

"Do; that is the best way."

Although he would fain have closed his weary eyes, the boy sat up and kept awake until his companion's plans were discussed for the morrow.

"I'll tell you what it is," Long Bob began: "we must make some arrangement about getting our living when we get to London. We cannot eat the paving-stones, neither can we sleep in the streets. Have you any idea yet?"

Jack said he had not.

"Well, I think," Long Bob said, "my best plan will be to find my old companions, and get a few coppers from them; enough, you know, to get us a shelter for the night. They will be sure to give me a little. Next day we must try and get a situation—there are always bills up for errand boys. Should we succeed, we can take a room for the little girl, and keep her all right; if not, we must hold horses, or sweep crossings—anything, you know, will be better than starving."

Poor Jack's heart sank. This was but a dismal picture, but he agreed with his companion that anything was better than starvation.

"I see you can scarcely keep your eyes open," Long Bob put in, "so suppose we go to sleep, and talk it over to-morrow."

His bedfellow gladly heard these words, and no sooner had he placed his head upon the pillow than he became lost to the outer world.

The boys were aroused by the hostess soon after daybreak, and descending to the kitchen they were regaled with a hearty breakfast.

Lily was with them, and the child looked brighter and happier than she had looked for many days. When the meal was over, Long Bob's pockets were made the receptacle for sufficient food to last them that day, and the kind-hearted woman, giving the boys a shilling each, wished them good-bye.

She kissed Lily at parting, and put a half-sovereign in her hand.

"God protect you," she said, holding the fair girl in her arms. "I hope you will soon be better off. Don't forget, my sweet child, if the worst comes to the worst, and you do not find a friend in the great London, that I will do all I can for you."

Lily promised never to forget Mrs. Mason, no matter what befell her, and returning the good woman's kiss, bade her Good bye, and ran after her companions.

This was the happiest morn they had known since they started from Falconmere, and when Long Bob was made acquainted with the present Lily had received, he threw his cap in the air and shouted with joy.

"Thirteen and threepence halfpenny," he said. "We are all right, Jack, for some days, and if our luck sticks to us we may both be doing something for a livelihood."

The journey that day seemed but a tenth part of the distance it was in reality, and when they entered the suburbs of London they were brought to a sudden standstill by Long Bob exclaiming—

"Oh! here's a treat. Two purfessinels eating bread and cheese."

The children turned and beheld the cause of Long Bob's remark, and that individual stuck his hands in his pockets, and grinned impudently at the two "purfessinels."

CHAPTER VIII.

BIG DRUM DISCOURSETH ON THE INGRATI-TUDE OF MANKIND.

THE "purfessinels," as Long Bob termed them, were not an uncommon sight to those whom business or pleasure caused to pass through the bye-streets of the great and many-peopled metropolis, and by them would have been passed without a second look.

To the children—one had been brought up among the gipsies, the other in the seclusion of Falconmere Abbey—the "purfessinels" were objects of more than ordinary interest.

Not so much on the men's part was this interest manifested as on the instruments of their vocation. A large drum, emblazoned with an impossible lion and an equally impossible animal with a single horn growing out of the centre of its forehead, stood on one corner of the table. Beside it one of those squeaking instruments, *vulgo* a mouth-organ, but which looked not unlike a dozen pieces of cane fastened together with several layers of wax-ends.

The men seated near the instruments were a study in themselves. The gentleman to whom the drum appertained was short, stout, and fat. A battered white hat with a black band was placed somewhat rakishly upon his head, and from beneath the rim two shreds of iron-grey hair were tastefully twisted into a form closely resembling the figure six.

His attire consisted of a seedy brown coat, seedier black, or, rather, once-had-been-black, trousers. Beyond this little else was seen, for the coat was closely buttoned over a blue spotted handkerchief; but whether to conceal the want of an under garment or to keep him warm was a matter that concerned only the individual himself.

But stay—his boots; they were, perhaps, the most peculiar part of his attire. The legs were Wellingtonians, and owing to a slight disarrangement with the bottoms of his trousers, the gap between the feet and calves was filled by the greasy brown legs of these lower coverings.

I pause and ask, Can I describe the soles of those boots? No, I cannot as I would wish. "Why?" you ask, courteous reader. I will tell you—because they were beyond my descriptive powers—far beyond.

In size they might have been fit coverings for the feet of Chang, in shape, anything you please.

The owner of these boots had, owing to circumstances over which he had no control, been compelled from time to time to restore their wasted constitution; he had, in fact, done his own "repairs neatly executed," and done it with a solidity which must have brought tears into the eyes of any son of Crispin who by chance saw them.

Many thicknesses of gutta percha had been glued on, and to strengthen this some fifty of the most formidable hobnails had been added; also a pair of heel tips, which would, upon an emergency, have shod a cob's fore-feet.

Big Drum, for so he was called (and no one knew whether it was his baptismal name or not), was proud of those boots, proud of his skill in the repairing line, and when he sat to rest or refresh himself the soles of his boots were always visible to the most casual observer; and he would indeed have been brave, in every sense of the word, could he have passed Big Drum's boot-soles unalarmed.

His companion, Pipes, was a direct contrast. He was tall, thin, and of the meekest temperament; he also had a habit—upon very cold days, when supplying the instructive

music during the time the company made a "pitch," and they often did so—it was then he would pause and use the fringed ends of his dirty comforter as most men use a pocket handkerchief.

Pipes also had boots which deserve a slight notice. They partook largely of the character of his carcase, being very long and narrow, and showing their meekness of disposition by turning up at the points, as though afraid to offend the stones by coming in contact with them.

Pipes' retiring, mild, bashful temperament formed as great a contrast to his friend's as the difference in their appearance. The latter had a forcible manner of impressing his companion with the truth of his remarks, and Pipes, having suffered from sundry hard knocks either with the ever-ready drumstick or any weapon that chanced to be within Big Drum's reach, had grown wise, and no matter how much he inwardly felt disposed to contradict his friend, he took especial care to outwardly assent.

When the young wanderers came to a standstill before the suburban public-house, the professionals were partaking of the humble, but hunger-satisfying fare, known as bread and cheese, "inguns," and porter.

Big Drum was in the act of finishing the last drop of the liquid, and sorrowfully regarding the maker's name on the bottom of the pewter measure—a scene caused by the absence of the necessary coin to refill the tankard.

He paused in the act, and Pipes did the same with respect to cutting off a piece of bread. The cheese and the fragments had long since disappeared, but Pipes, who believed that crust was good for the digestion, was determined to finish his share of the loaf.

"I told you," said Big Drum, the pewter measure within an inch of his lips, "that we should meet with luck."

"Where?" Pipes asked. "Where's the luck?"

"It's come to us—it's here. Look there!"

Pipes looked, and beheld the trio, and mildly cutting off the corner of his piece of bread, remarked—

"Tramps."

"Yes," Big Drum said, "tramps; perhaps they is. I hope so."

"Do you? Why?"

"I'll tell you why, Pipes. If they is tramps, our fortin's made. Look at the figger of that gal!"

Pipes did so.

"A werry grand figger," he said; "but I don't see how it can make our fortins."

Big Drum placed the measure upon the table without finishing the remains of the pot of porter, and said, just loud enough for Pipes to hear—

"Them two boys in tights, and the gal in muslin and beautiful plumes, how would they look, eh? Do you see now?"

Pipes nodded, placed his knife and piece of bread upon the table, took up the quart measure, lifted it, gave a sigh, and answered—

"Yes, if they'd do it."

"Do it?" Big Drum said. "In course they will."

Pipes gazed reflectively at the inside of the empty measure, and said—

"P'rhaps. I hopes they will."

Big Drum set his hat straight, and looking towards the children, said—

"Well, my little dears, you seems to have come a long way. Ain't you tired?"

"Not very," said Long Bob. "Why do you ask?"

"Because," Big Drum said, insinuatingly, "I is fond of children, and—and—can't you come and set down for a minnit and take a rest? I'll stand a pot of——"

He paused as a thought of the exchequer came to his mind, and shifting towards Pipes, nearly pushed that worthy from his seat, as he made room for the children beside him.

Jack Lennox went boldly forward, holding Lily by the hand; they were both tired, and glad of an opportunity to rest.

Long Bob sat himself upon the edge of the table, and took up Pipes' instrument, and began to discourse sweet music therefrom.

Pipes mildly took it from him, and asked—

"Would you like to be a musician, young man?"

"Should not mind," was the answer; "anything would be welcome just now."

Big Drum brought his fist down upon the table, and exclaimed joyfully—

"Thought so! Will you join the purfession?"

There was the faintest smile upon Long Bob's lips as he answered—

"I shouldn't mind if you could take my companions as well."

"Take 'em—take 'em?" Big Drum said, gleefully, "in course I can; the very thing. Talk about the Buffler and the paper pole, they would be nothin' agin you three."

"Should say not," remarked Bob, although he had not the most remote idea of the meaning of Big Drum's words; "that little girl would draw more coppers than all the bufflers in——Hallo!"

Big Drum, carried away by the excitement of the moment, seized Long Bob by the hand, and began to shake it violently.

He did the same with Lily and Jack, and wound up by slapping Pipes upon the back, and saying—

"I told you so—a regular fortin."

The heavy hand drove all the breath from Pipes' thin form, and he could only make furtive attempts at an answer—attempts that failed until he wiped the tears from his eyes with the end of his scarf, then he managed to gasp out—

"I knows you did."

Big Drum went into the heart of the business at once. He made a proposal, and our little friends joyfully accepted what they believed would be a career of unalloyed happiness.

Long Bob was in ecstasies at the prospect Big Drum held out, and he longed for the hour to come when an admiring audience would behold him holding a ten-feet pole, or performing wondrous evolutions with the brass balls.

He fairly yelled with delight at the idea of the skin-tight suit Big Drum promised to procure.

"Now, my dears," the manager of this company said, "suppose we has a little drop o' summut to settle the bargain, then pack up our traps and—— What are you doing, you shadder?"

This question was addressed to Pipes, who brought the sharp edge of his square-toed boot in contact with Big Drum's shin.

Pipes brought his mouth close to his companion's ear and whispered—

"Wot's the use of talking about having summut by way of a clincher? Did not I spend the last blessed coin in that 'ere pot o' beer?"

Big Drum rubbed his red nose until it assumed a polish painful to behold, then thrust his hands in his empty pockets.

"Right, Pipes," he said. "We ain't very flush just now, so we'll put the treat off till arter the first night of our performance. You ain't hungry, my dears, are you?"

They told him they were not.

"I'm glad of that, cos, under present circumstances, it would be inconvenient to be hungry; but what are we to do for a turn-in to-night? I wish we could give a performance at once, but we can't; and I'm blowed if I knows how we shall manage to live till you three gets well up in the purfession."

Long Bob laughed.

"I s'pose," said Big Drum, "you don't think it a purfession. That shows how little you knows of the world, young man. Wot's the difference atween me and Pipes doing the music and you two performing, to a lot of fiddlers a scraping away and fellows doing the climbing business a top of each other's shoulders on the boards? We does it on the boards—at least you will, though your boards won't be inside a place all lighted up, and men and women a drinking and smoking. No, ours is the true purfes-

gion. Buffler said so, and he knowed a thing or two."

Pipes, who had been sadly contemplating the empty measures, looked up when Big Drum came to this part of his speech, and in a sepulchral voice, said—

"The Buffler did know a thing or two, cuss him!"

He gave a deep-drawn sigh, then relapsed again to the study of the name stamped on the bottom of the pewter measure.

"That reminds me," Big Drum said, "I must tell you about the Buffler, and I hopes his conduct will be a warning to you all. You see Pipes there, and you see me, Big Drum?"

They answered in the affirmative.

"Well," he resumed, "you sees two victims of ingratitude—about the worst ingratitude as ever you or anybody ever heard of."

Big Drum shook his head, and came to a dead stop.

"When I thinks of it," he said, after a moment's thought, "I feels that the beasts of the forest is better than men is one to another—much better—and all I hope is you won't do as the Buffler did, that's all."

"What did he do?" Long Bob asked.

"Do?" Big Drum said. "Do? I'll tell you what he done. He bolted, sir—yes, bolted, after all the trouble and expense me and Pipes was at to teach him his purfession."

"Bolted? I suppose you mean he parted company with you?"

"Parted company?" Big Drum looked fiercely at Pipes, but as the latter was deep in the study of the lion's fore-legs—the impossible lion on the drum—he had no excuse to wreak his vengeance upon his mild and inoffensive partner. "Parted company? Yes, he did, but that was not all. I wish it had been; but I'll tell you how it took place, then you'll be able to judge if the Buffler wasn't the most ungratefullest wagabone in the world."

Pipes, in a melancholy voice—

"He was."

"Nobody asked you to put your spoke in," Big Drum said fiercely: "hadn't it been for you he wouldn't have come over us as he did."

Pipes subsided, and began this time to examine the unicorn.

"I say," Long Bob said, "we have come a long way, and if you don't look sharp with your story we shall not be able to get a lodging to-night."

"That's true, young man, so I will begin."

Lily and Jack drew closer to their new friend, both anxious to hear the nature of the offence of which the Buffler had been guilty.

"It was this," Big Drum said, "when Pipes and I began to perform together we met the Buffler. He was a smart-looking sort of chap, and a good figger. He wanted to join us, and we let him; but, blow yer, he was no more fit to do his part than that table is to throw a summersault.

"Well, Pipes and I—not as Pipes did much, you know—we taught the Buffler, and I can tell you he came out properly, and used to draw the coppers like one o'clock."

"What did he do?" Long Bob asked, anxious to emulate, if possible, the clever but ungrateful Buffler.

"Do?" Big Drum said, "why, hanythink; he could do a break-down or a hornpipe, balance a pole on his feet, and throw the balls to rights."

Long Bob sighed; the prospective greatness was almost too much for him.

He heard with inward awe Big Drum's account of the Buffler's skill, and wondered if the time would come when his performance would merit such warm encomiums.

"Well, he stayed with us a long time, he did," Big Drum continued, "till at last we began to think about opening a hexibition, and showing off the Buffler as the Vaulting Lion of Bagdad."

Pipes here rubbed his nose with the fringe of his necktie, and whispered the faintest possible whisper by the way—

"That was my title."

Big Drum faced round suddenly; so suddenly that Pipes edged away until he edged himself off his seat, and fell to the ground, clutching, in his attempt to save himself, the drum.

The light instrument came with a bang upon his head, and Big Drum, in agony, sprang to his feet, snatched one of the drumsticks from the ground, and before Pipes could escape began to belabour him.

"Who said it wasn't your title?" remarked the angry owner of the fallen drum; "is that any reason you is to upset my instrument and knock it out of tune, you horrible shadder? Now I tells you, once for all, that if ever you puts your spoke in when you're not wanted you'll get more than you like."

The children were convulsed with laughter at the scene, and when Big Drum, making a furious blow at Pipes, caught his knuckles on the edge of the table, Long Bob rolled on the ground, well-nigh suffocated with merriment.

The blow caused the weapon to fly from Big Drum's fingers, and while he danced about in pain Pipes crawled away to a place of safety.

It was some time before order was restored, and Big Drum could be induced to resume his story. When he did so, he said—

"We should have got up the hexibition, only we was waiting to get together a little coin to begin. Every day we used to put away a little, and yesterday we had altogether, in a leather bag, two pun two and fourpence a'penny."

Big Drum paused, cast his eyes up to the sky, then closed his fist, and glanced round as though he was in search of the ungrateful Buffler.

"We had all this," he resumed, "and last night as ever was Pipes there let the Buffler go round with the bag to collect."

"I did," groaned Pipes. "I wish I hadn't."

"It ain't any use a whinin' over it now," said Big Drum savagely. "You'd no business to let him go round at all. I always told you that."

"I know you did. Oh, Lord! when I thinks of that two pun' two and fourpence ha'penny, I feels dreadful."

Big Drum turned away from his unfortunate partner, and, addressing his young listeners, said—

"He went round to collect—cuss him, the wagabone! To think, after all the trouble that I took with him to make him a 'purfessionel,' the dress I bought him, and—and—after all this, and a lot more we done for him, he—he collected the coin, then bolted—yes, bolted, bag and all, and a whole box of properties—three beautiful brass balls, a dagger, ten hoops, and the beautiful pole he used to draw out of his mouth after eating paper—all these went along with the Buffler and the bag."

Big Drum ceased, his eyes closed, and pulling his battered hat over his forehead he gave a groan.

Pipes groaned in sympathy, and cast a melancholy glance at the bright, but empty pewter measure. It was too much to remember without grieving both in the spirit and most terribly loud.

"Buffler—two pun' two and fourpence ha'penny!" this said Pipes to himself. "Oh, dear! oh, dear! the ungrateful wretch."

"Two pun' two and the odd ha'pence," groaned Big Drum, "and the beautiful lot of properties. Oh! I shall die! Not a penny in my pocket to begin a new company."

"I say," Long Bob said, after quietly surveying the sorrowful pair, "don't pile up the agony too much. We have a few shillings; leaving as much as will get the little girl a bed, you are welcome to the rest, if it will set us going in the new line."

"How much is it?" Big Drum asked.

"Yes, how much?" queried Pipes, in a sepulchral whisper.

"Thirteen and threepence ha'penny," said Long Bob.

Big Drum opened his mouth twice before he could speak. When able to articulate, he gasped out—

"Bless you, my boy, bless you! I can see you will not serve us as the Buffler did—generous, noble youth!"

"No fear," Long Bob said; "you act square by us, and we'll do the same by you."

When Pipes heard the magnificent sum mentioned, he rubbed his nose with the dirty worsted fringe, and clutching the smaller of the pewter measures, whispered—

"Borrow a shilling, Drum; borrow a shilling to begin with.

Big Drum acted upon the suggestion, and Long Bob supplied the money, one-third of which went to refill the pewter measure.

Talking over their future plans, the party sat until night came on. As talking was apt to affect Big Drum's lungs, he managed to borrow two shillings more from the little Lily's purse; and when this had been expended they arose, Big Drum promising to take them to a cheap but respectable lodging at the east end of London.

Pipes was so overcome by the recollection of the Buffler's perfidy, that when he was called to accompany his companions, they beheld him shedding tears over the pewter measure, and giving vent to his grief in audible, but disconnected sentences.

"The Buffler—hic," he sobbed, "two pun'—hic—brass balls—hic—bolted—good young man, lent us three shillings—hic—hic—bolted with the bag—hic—ungrateful rascal—all Big—ig—Drum's—hic—fault."

They detached him from the object of his solicitude, and got him to his feet; but even then the recollection of the Buffler's villany was too strong for him to forget easily—so strong, in fact, that he rolled from side to side, and would have fallen had not Big Drum supported him.

So they entered the great city, and on the morrow they were to begin a new phase in their strange and eventful career.

CHAPTER IX.

A STRANGE STORY.

SOON after the condemned gipsy had been led to his cell, a warder of the prison waited upon the governor, and told him that a gentleman wished for a few moments' interview upon a matter of the greatest importance.

The governor gave the necessary permission for the stranger to pass the grim portal of the prison.

A tall, distinguished-looking man entered the governor's private room soon after the warder had disappeared.

His face was bronzed by the sun of other climes, and his long beard and jetty hair were tinged with white.

In years, he was yet young; but there was an expression of such deep melancholy upon his frank face which told how deeply he had suffered.

He bowed with stately grace to the governor, and seating himself in the proffered chair, said—

"I have ventured to visit you, sir, with the hope that you will, although I know it is out of the usual course of prison matters, grant me an interview with the man who was yesterday sentenced to transportation for entering Earl Falconmere's bedchamber."

The governor looked surprised, and mentally wondered what connection could exist between the visitant and the felon gipsy.

The governor had, during his term of office, seen many strange things, and had become the depositary of many strange and awful secrets; thus his request did not cause him a second's thought.

"Of course you have weighty reasons for making this request?"

"I have," was the answer, and the finely chiselled lips twitched nervously as he spoke; "very weighty reasons."

"I merely asked," the governor said, "because many have preferred the same request merely to gratify a morbid curiosity. Criminals," he added, "become objects of the most tender solicitude to many; therefore, in granting a similar request to yours, I have to be careful. You can understand. It is not pleasant to read an account in the next day's paper, published by one of those meddling, ill-judging people."

The stranger smiled.

"My errand," he said, "is soon explained. That man alone can clear up a mystery, the very shadow of which casts such a blight upon my existence that, but for the hope of finding my boy, I should care but little how soon I lay beneath the earth."

The governor became interested in his visitor, not so much from his words, but by his manner.

"If I remember," he said, "the convict told a most improbable story before the judge. Has your visit any reference to this?"

"It has; the helpless girl whose death he described was my wife, Earl Falconmere's daughter."

"Great heavens! Yet the earl told the court that his daughter was buried two years before the woman spoken of by the gipsy appeared at the Abbey gate."

"He lied," said the stranger. "She was alive at the time he mentioned, and with me in Italy."

"Your evidence," said the governor, "to support the gipsy's story will be a serious matter for the earl."

"He is dead."

"Dead?" repeated the governor. "Impossible!"

"He was destroyed last night by the fall of the Abbey walls—perished miserably amid the flames of his proud home—and Heaven has saved my hand from being red with the vengeance I swore to wreak upon the destroyer of my wife."

There was a long pause, then the governor spoke.

"Was there not," he asked, "a boy belonging to the unfortunate lady?"

"There was. It is of him I wish to hear. Heaven send he may yet be left me!"

The governor, before they parted, heard a sad story from the bronzed stranger's lips, and when he left him at the door of the gipsy's cell, the kindly old man's heart was heavier than its wont.

The gipsy received his visitor with a scowling countenance; but when he gave utterance to a name he had heard from the suicide's lips, he sprang from his seat, and exclaimed—

"You are Walter Carlin! then I am saved from the horrors of a convict settlement."

"I will do all in my power," the stranger said; "but we will talk of that anon. Tell me of my boy."

"He is with the tribe, and will be given up to you when I am free and avenged."

"You are avenged."

"How? By your coming? That is not—"

"Earl Falconmere," said the tall stranger, "is dead."

The gipsy uttered a shout of joy.

"Dead!" he exclaimed, "dead! Slain by the hands of my people!"

"He perished amid the flames of his ancestral home."

"They did the work well," said the gipsy, calmly. "Now, Captain Carlin, I will tell you all you wish to know."

Our hero's father seated himself upon the side of the convict's pallet, and with an anguished expression upon his face, listened to the gipsy's story.

"It is now nearly nine years," he said, "since I found a bare-footed, broken-hearted woman, bent down with want and suffering, dragging her weary limbs through a lonely road that leads to Falconmere Abbey. She, though scarcely able to stand, had a child of some four years old in her arms.

"I saw the poor creature staggering beneath her burden, and offered to assist her— an offer she gladly accepted, and together we entered the gates of the proud domain. But little conversation passed between us, although I saw that the poor sufferer's attire, though at the time torn and ragged, was of far different material to that which usually clothed the houseless mendicant. I also noted that her hands were white, and of a shape that ill-accorded with her condition ; yet, in spite of these things, I was dazed and stupified when she announced herself to be the only child of Falconmere's proud earl.

"I will not weary you with the details of that sad journey, sir," the gipsy continued, his voice now tremulous and touchingly pathetic, "nor will I repeat the story of suffering and misery I heard from the trembling lips, but pass on to the time when we stood cowering before one of her father's liveried menials. She, the daughter of a peer, had the door closed in her face ; then she pleaded for an interview with her parent. The low plaintive voice yet sounds in my ear, when she sent her message to that stern, unforgiving man, who now dares to lift his head in the bright sun, and takes his place among the lawgivers of his country.

"'Tell him,' she said, 'that I have come to ask his forgiveness before I die—to see him—once more, if only for a moment.'

"The man conveyed her supplicating wish to her relentless sire, and soon returned with orders to drive the mendicant from the door. The earl, said the man, had but one child, and she was dead, and her corpse could be seen in the family vault. He concluded by telling the poor shivering woman, that unless she quitted the precincts of the Abbey, he would have her placed in the stocks as a vagrant.

"Though crushed for a moment by this brutal answer, the poor girl, as she clung to the doorway for support, reiterated her words, and taking a packet of papers from her breast, bade the lacquey convey them to the unnatural being with whom she claimed affinity.

"Never shall I forget the look of frenzy that gleamed from the suppliant eyes when the man returned and told her that the earl had destroyed what he termed a packet of forged letters. She snatched the child from my arms, and, without a word, fled from the home of her childhood.

"I followed her as quickly as the darkness would permit, and I came up with her as she reached a deep pool of water. She paused upon the brink, and turned fiercely upon me. I saw her purpose, and sought to save her, but only succeeded in tearing the child from her maddened grasp ; the next moment she was beneath the dark waters, held down by the weeds and rank grass that grew beneath.

"I took the boy to our camp, and tended him as though he had been my own child, and next morning we placed the poor drowned woman in her grave. Soon after we left this part of the country, and only returned a few weeks previous to my apprehension.

"Although so many years had passed, the boy's wrongs were not forgotten by our tribe, and I waited upon the earl to endeavour to soften his heart towards our *protégé*. His answer was an utter denial of the relationship, and I was driven like a dog from the Abbey." The gipsy's eyes flashed at the remembrance of this indignity, and clenching his hands upon the rail before him, he added—"This, in place of causing me to desist from my purpose, had quite a contrary effect. I determined, that moment, to obtain possession of the proofs necessary to carry out my plan.

"These proofs I knew were to be found in the packet of papers which the earl retained upon that night when his daughter found a resting-place beneath the dark waters of the pool. I felt assured that they were not destroyed, and twice previous to the night I was taken I entered the Abbey, and searched among the papers in the earl's library. Upon each occasion my search was fruitless, and I determined to return once more, and open a large escritoire I had seen in the bed-chamber. You are aware of the result of that enterprise."

He ceased speaking, and the brave officer who had faced death in the red field of strife, bowed his head in his hands and wept like a child.

CHAPTER X.

BIG DRUM HOLDS A GRAND REHEARSAL.

UPON the strength of the new company Big Drum rented a large room (upon credit) for the twofold purpose of sleeping and rehearsal. Lily, who was a favourite with the landlady of the house, had by this means a very small but clean room for her sole use.

It is true, when these arrangements were completed, there was a slight hitch respecting the commissariat department ; but this difficulty Drum likewise overcame.

A chandler's shop, where he had been wont to purchase the staple articles of food, *i.e.*, bread and cheese, was visited, and owing to Big Drum's eloquence, the shopman agreed to supply the necessary provender until a performance should recruit the exchequer.

These matters settled, the rehearsals began in earnest.

A brother professional, now retired, and sole proprietor of a fish shop, sold his box of properties to Big Drum (he gave three weeks' credit), and to Drum's delight there was an old suit—partly clown, the remainder indescribable—in this valuable collection.

The suit fitted Long Bob, save a few alterations ; these Pipes made, and, much to his self-gratulation, Mr. Robert Jawkins was permitted to appear in "tights" upon the third rehearsal.

Pipes wept tears of joy when he beheld Long Bob's manner of throwing the gilt balls in the air. But when he beheld our long friend lying on his back, his feet elevated, and balancing a painted pole eight feet long, he gave a sepulchral laugh and faintly whispered—

"Beats the Buffler into nothing!"

"Should say it does," Long Bob answered, as he spun the pole round with marvellous swiftness. "Could the Buffler do this?"

Pipes was much affected, and shaking his head, murmured—

"Couldn't touch it. You is a regular fortin, that you is."

Big Drum made no remark, he was happy.

Seated upon an inverted apple-basket, he rubbed the tip of his fiery nose until it looked red-hot.

When Long Bob had concluded, Jack Lennox took his place ; the boy's lithe, muscular form seemed like india-rubber as he went through a number of postures suggested by Big Drum.

Balancing himself upon his right foot, he extended his left, keeping the leg straight ; then grasping his ankle, he spun round like a teetotum, a feat which caused the quiet Pipes to gently clap his hands and whisper—

"Bravo!"

He would have uttered it aloud, but Big Drum sat so still, his hands upon his knees, and his head craned forward, watching breathlessly the handsome boy's movements. Pipes was in too much dread of his impulsive companion to disturb him.

Jack wound up by throwing his hands backwards, and bending his body until his fingers touched his heels ; then springing upward, he turned a somersault and came upon his feet.

"Brayvo!" shouted Big Drum. "There ain't a Buffler in the world as could do that."

"There ain't," came in a whisper from the corner.

"Now, my little lady," Big Drum lovingly said to Lily, "it is your turn. Don't forget to spin round when you finishes the dance. Play up, Pipes."

The melancholy one fumbled in his pocket, and brought forth his instrument of torture ; then wiping his lips with the fringe of his scarf he began assassinating the Great Eastern Polka.

The graceful child's figure looked to advantage as she went through her part, a feat she embellished with so much innate grace and elegance that Big Drum and Pipes both exclaimed, when it was over—

"She'll draw, she will."

Long Bob desisted for a moment in his frantic attempts to balance a long feather on the tip of his nose, and answered—

"Draw! Should say so, too. Why, the browns 'll jump out of the people's pockets when she does the whirligig."

This was Long Bob's term for the pirouette with which Lily conncluded her performance.

"Hopes they will," said Pipes—"hopes they will."

"I expect," Long Bob said, giving up the feather business as too much at present, "that you will have to make that box of yours bigger to hold the coin."

Pipes hoped so too, and wrapping his mouth-organ carefully in brown paper, he went to the cupboard and brought the viands to the table.

The young trio were hungry ; and though the bread was stale and the cheese in form like a cannon-ball, in substance a close imitation of bees'-wax, they partook of it with as much gusto as an alderman would a civic dinner.

Jack Lennox went for the beer, and when he returned he somewhat startled the party by exclaiming—

"Tinker Tom is at the end of the court."

A bomb-shell dropped upon the table could not have created more confusion than these words did.

Long Bob ran to the fire-place and seized the poker ; Pipes drew forth his instrument, but whether to charm the savage breast by playing upon it, or to use it as a weapon of offence, must remain a mystery.

Big Drum, a drum-stick in each hand, placed his burly form before the door, and heroically said—

"Let him come."

Lily ran and nestled close to Jack Lennox, and the boy, passing one arm around her waist, whispered—

"Fear not, Lily ; he shall never take you from me."

Thus they stood for several seconds, and Long Bob, finding that Tinker Tom did not ascend the stairs, placed the poker in the grate and said—

"There's a tabloo! Bravo Drum! you looks like 'Ajacks' a defying the moon, only he didn't wear his hat on the back of his chump."

Big Drum certainly looked peculiar.

His broad back was placed against the door, his hands, clutching the drum-sticks, were above his head, and his face was turned towards the children expressive of the greatest dismay.

He fully imagined that Tinker Tom had come to rob him of his prospective fortune, and determined to resist to the last.

The children had told the story of their escape from Falconmere, and the danger likely to accrue should Tinker Tom discover them. Thus the mention of his name was sufficient to cause a panic among the embryo professionals.

Long Bob's remark brought them to their seats again, then Jack Lennox, placing his hand upon Bob's wrist, said correctively—

"Ajax defied the lightning, Bob, not the moon."

"Did he? Well, it would have served him right if the light—— Hallo, there, Pipes! What are you up to?"

Pipes was quietly sewing a large parti-coloured rosette on the breast of Long Bob's dress, when this interrogation so startled him that he ran the point of the needle in his thumb.

"I ain't doin' anythink."

"Except," said Long Bob, "making a horful ugly face. What's the matter?"

"Pricked my thumb."

"Serve you right. Why didn't you let my dress alone?"

"I wish I had," said Pipes, dolefully.

Lily and Jack were deprived of the pleasure they had hitherto experienced in accompanying Long Bob upon a ramble after rehearsal; the knowledge that Tinker Tom was upon their trail was sufficient to keep them within the house.

"Never mind," said Long Bob; "you will see plenty of London the day after to-morrow."

He spoke of the time fixed upon for their first appearance before the public; and, child-like, Lily clapped her hands joyfully.

"Only one day more, then I shall wear that beautiful frock Mrs. Smith has been making. Have you seen it, Jack?"

"No," he said; "I believe I have been too much engrossed with the preparation of my own costume."

"It's very beautiful," she said; "and poor Pipes, what patience he must have had to put all those pretty shining dots all over your dress."

"Yes, Lil, he has been very kind; but do you know I don't think he is very happy."

They were standing at the open window, out of hearing of their companions, who were employed in various ways in preparing for the great *début*.

Big Drum was renovating his instrument by pipe-claying the cords; rubbing, or trying to rub, several suspicious-looking dark circles from the parchment. People who were not particular in their remarks would have said these rings were tell-tale marks left by the various foaming pewter measures that had been placed thereon, when the Buffler and prosperity smiled upon Drum.

Pipes was busy with a flat-iron and a damp piece of cloth, taking the indentations out of his hat. A necessary repair, for, as Long Bob said, the battered tile bore a close resemblance to a concertina bellows than aught else.

The last-named gentleman had his share of the work. What little instruction he had received from the little tailor came in very useful upon the present occasion, and in a very creditable manner he repaired sundry rents in Big Drum and Pipes' garments.

Pipes was not idle; coiled round the fore finger of his right hand was a wet piece of flannel, and in a soft and melancholy manner he was washing the faces of the impossible lion and the equally impossible unicorn. Both animals seemed much refreshed by the operation.

Lily turned her head towards the wild beast cleaner, and said—

"Pipes not happy, Jack? Why do you think so?"

"He seems so quiet, Lil—so different to Big Drum, that I often wonder how they came together; but," he said, suddenly changing the subject, "I want to ask you a question, Lily."

He had his arm round her waist, and her head, with its golden shower, was lying upon his shoulder.

"Is it," she asked, "a very serious question, Jack?"

"Serious! Why, do I look so?"

"You do."

"Well," he said, "it is a little serious. I want to know whether you like this life we are about to enter upon?"

She paused a moment before answering him, then shaking her head somewhat sadly, said—

"I should have liked better to have stayed at Falconmere; but now poor papa is gone, and we have not a friend in the world, what can we do? We shall starve, unless we go out to perform. I would sooner do anything than be hungry again. You know how dreadful it was when I had to pick up a raw turnip and eat it."

Jack's eyes filled with tears at the recollection of that miserable day, and, in a voice somewhat husky and low, he said—

"Yes, it was dreadful, Lil; and at present we can do nothing except follow in the path chance has opened. Something better may be our lot some day, until then we must be content."

The brave little fellow knew too well that the mode they were about to follow of obtaining a living would be one of toil; but, with the hope that fortune would yet be kinder to them, he nerved himself to face the battle of life with a degree of fortitude that would have well become one older and more experienced in the world's ways.

JACK LENNOX RESCUES LILLY FROM THE VIOLENCE OF TINKER TOM.

From the present and future their conversation turned to the unexpected appearance of Tinker Tom.

"I wonder," Jack said, "how he could have followed us so closely, Lil; we have not been in London a week, and he is close upon us."

Lily shuddered.

She had an instinctive dread of that dark, vengeful man—a dread that had wound itself around her heart until his very name caused her faculties to become deadened and her spirit to sink, as though a heavy sorrow was upon her.

Poor child! Was it that her peculiar organization foretold that the gipsy would prove a crushing blight upon her early life—that his coming was like an evil shadow in her path? If so, the secret workings of her fears were not groundless, for the man was destined to become all her worst fears portrayed.

"It may have been chance that brought him here," she said, in answer to Jack's words; "yet something tells me that he will yet attempt to carry out the dreadful plan you overheard. He shall not," she added, with a determination that was singular in one so young; "I will never become what he would make me—never."

Jack Lennox's face reddened, and closing his small hands, he answered—

"Tinker Tom shall not have you, Lily. His appearance here has warned us of our danger. Though I cannot protect you, Big Drum can. I wish," he added, "my strength would enable me to cope with him. But never mind, Lil, some day I shall have more; then let Tinker Tom or any one else look out that dares to look at you."

Lily smiled at her companion's warmth.

"I know you would," she said. "You are a brave fellow, Jack, and I like you very much."

His eyes sparkled brightly.

"Do you," he asked, "really like me, Lil? like the poor ragged gipsy boy who—"

She placed her hand over his mouth, and adroitly changed the conversation by saying—

"It was lucky we told Big Drum all about our escape from the gipsies. He will know best what to do should Tinker Tom ever meet us in the street."

"Better than we should, Lil. I hope we shall not meet him."

"I hope not."

"Hullo, there, you two!"

The young pair turned and beheld Long Bob coming towards them, holding at arm's length the flesh-coloured continuations which he had been altering for Jack Lennox.

"Here, Jack," he continued; "here is your tights; take care of them—they'll fit now."

Jack and Lily were loud in their praises of Bob's skill in thus producing such a glittering dress—praises which R. J. received in his usual modest manner.

"They ain't bad," he said. "I think if I had stopped long enough with my thirsty master I should have done pretty well, eh?"

"You would, indeed, Bob. Why, no one could tell, surely, that so many places had to be darned—"

"Fine drawn, if you please, Jack."

"Yes; I had forgotten—fine drawn. They look like new."

"Better than new," R. J. said. "New ones might shrink—these won't."

"How is that, Bob?"

"They have been washed too often—ha, ha, ha!"

"What are you laughing about?"

"Look at Pipes."

They turned and saw the poor fellow in evident tribulation.

He had been busy with the repairs necessary to render his boots worthy of the great appearance they were about to make; for this purpose he had melted various pieces of gutta-percha to stop a leakage in the soles, but, owing to an absence of the necessary tools, he had run the hot solution on the back of his hand in place of the damaged boot soles.

Big Drum looked up when his companion's cry of pain sounded upon his ears, and asked—

"What's the matter, shadder?"

"Ugh!" gasped Pipes. "Been and put the hot gutta-percha on my hand instead of the boots."

"Ha, ha, ha!" laughed Big Drum. "The gutta-percha know'd where it was most wanted. Keep it there, Pipes; people will think you've got fat. Ha, ha, ha!"

Long Bob came to the rescue, and detached the warm protuberances from Pipes' hand. Beyond an inflamed appearance upon the skin there was not much the matter.

"To-morrow, ladies and gentlemen," Big Drum said, when Pipes had subsided into the darkest corner of the room, "there will be a full-dress rehearsal of the company arter breakfust, that is, if the togs are all ready."

"Properties all ready," said Long Bob, gravely, "except the stage, that ain't visible."

"Ah!" Big Drum rubbed his nose reflectively. "That's an unfortunate circumstance, and I'm blow'd if I knows what's to be done about it. Pipes!"

A whisper from the corner answered—

"Yes."

"We ain't got no stage, Pipes ; what's to be done ? "

" Steal a shutter as we go along," was the answer.

" You're a disgrace to the purfession," said Big Drum, severely. "How can we steal one when the people keeps 'em down the gratings in front of the shops ? "

" I know," Long Bob said. " I know how to get one."

" How, Bob ? "

" Let's go out to-night ; while you burke the boy that pulls the shutters up, I'll cut away with it."

" Young man," said Big Drum, " did you ever go to school ? "

" Should say I did."

" Where ? "

" That," Long Bob said, " is a question I cannot answer at present. Not as I think you'd split on me, but the people at the large academy where I was educated are so lost without my presence that they will give a suvrin reward for my apprehension."

" I don't want to know anything about that," said Drum. "But if you went to school you used copy books."

" Four," Long Bob said. " I dare say I should have had more only the tailors wanted a lad of genius to invent something new."

" Did you ever, when you wrote, see a line on the top of one of the pages, which said, ' Honesty is the way to be rich ? ' "

" Can't say I did."

" Perhaps it wasn't in your books, but you have seen another line, which said, ' Evil manners corrupt good communications.' "

Long Bob laughed until the tears came to his eyes.

" You've put the cart afore the horse, Drum," he said. " Yes, I've seen that one. What about it ? "

" This, young man. Your evil man——"

" Communications, Drum."

" Communications, then ! "

Big Drum was getting savage.

" Will corrupt the good manners of that well-bred little boy and the little girl ; so if you can't think of anything better than burking a boy and running away with the shutter, all I have to say is——"

Bang !

The drum-head, which had been too much tightened while the parchment was wet, cracked, and the report startled the party, and stayed the manager's lecture.

Unhappy Pipes, as usual, met with the warmest thanks from the owner of the instrument.

" I know'd it," said Drum—" I know'd it. I told you not to go washing them lions in the coat-of-arms. There, that's wot comes of your meddling, you shadder of ill-luck.

I'm a good mind to smash you, I am. No stage was bad enough—no music wusser."

" It's not my fault," whispered Pipes, as he dodged under the table. " I didn't touch the parchment."

" It's your fault, I tell you again, and don't answer me, or it will be wuss for you. Oh, lord ! oh, lord ! No stage, nor no music, all through you."

Pipes' nose was just visible beyond the leg of the table, as he, in a whisper, louder and firmer than usual, said—

" It ain't my fault, then, and I don't care what you say ; as for music, ain't we got my instrument ? It's a good job it was bust, people will be able to hear the notes when I play. They couldn't do it when that horrid thing was banging like a——"

This was adding insult to injury with a vengeance. So Big Drum thought, for he gave a yell, and seizing Pipes by the collar dragged him from beneath the table, and while shaking the offender with all his strength, he growled—

" Good job, was it—good job ! That just explains the accident. So you—you mean wretch, you did it because you wanted to do all the music yourself."

" No, I didn't."

" You did—your own words prove it. Your notes ! What's that squeaking thing to do with the performance at all ? Where would you be without the drum ? Don't it bring a audience together ? Don't it make the performers go through their work better, eh ? Answer me, you shadder, or—or I'll——"

" That'll do, Drum," said Long Bob ; "don't shake him like that. It wasn't his fault ; it was yours."

Big Drum released his captive, and turned towards Bob, and rubbing his nose in a slow and calm manner, answered—

" This is too much, you to turn ag'in me. Ain't it enough that we are—there—there, young man, I am not surprised ; after the Buffler's most ungrateful conduct, anything wouldn't be too much."

" Look here, Drum," Bob said. " Now, listen to reason. How could Pipes do that ? Just tell me how he could do it."

Big Drum pointed to the break in the parchment, and dolefully said—

" Look ! ain't it busted ? Do you think I'd do it ? "

" Certainly not ; but never mind, I'll soon sew it up, and it will be as good as ever again."

He did so ; and Drum, after testing the sound, was affected almost to tears.

The music being all right again, a council was held about the shutter before mentioned, and to the delight of all, Long Bob got over the difficulty.

"I'll tell you what," he said ; "there's the very thing down stairs."

"Where ? " asked Big Drum, joyfully.

"Mrs. Smith uses it for a shutter in the kitchen. Wait a moment, I'll go and ask her to lend it us."

He went ; and Big Drum, now restored to good-temper, turned to Pipes, saying—

"That young man, Pipes, is a fortin in himself."

"He is," said Pipes, who bore no malice for the recent attack Big Drum had made upon him—"a regular fortin. Beats the Buffler into fits."

"The Buffler," said Big Drum, "is no-where. This young man, though his legs might be a bit straighter, is better than forty Bufflers."

The subject of this remark entered the room staggering under the weight of a shutter, which Mrs. Smith had been prevailed upon to lend them.

"Here it are," said Bob ; "she wouldn't lend it at first ; but I told her, unless we got it we couldn't go out, so she wouldn't get her rent. That touched the old gal—she let me have it in no time."

The shutter was placed in the centre of the room, and Big Drum, after trying its firmness, went back to his seat, and rubbing his hands, said complacently—

"Here, this is all right now, so to-morrow we will have a full dress rehearsal ; the day after we will start."

"Yes," whispered Pipes, "and I shall be glad when we do ; here's four days, and I haven't seen the colour of a coin. I say, Bob."

"Well, old 'un."

"Do you think Mrs. Smith would mind lending us a shilling ? "

"What for ? "

Pipes placed his mouth close to Long Bob's ear and whispered—

"To get some beer."

"Pipes," said Big Drum, "I'm ashamed of you. Can't you wait until we has coin of our own to get what you want ? You are a disgrace to our purfession ; you always was, Pipes."

"I'm blest if his ears ain't as sharp as a rat's," mentally remarked Pipes. "Who'd a thought of his hearing that ? "

A few alterations were made in the con-struction of the shutter so kindly lent by Mrs. Smith. This done, Big Drum said everything was as right as ninepence, and like his company, prepared for the grand rehearsal on the morrow.

The time came, and much to the edifica-tion of the lady and her two ragged children who lived beneath the manager's room, the rehearsal began.

The shutter was placed in the middle of the floor ; Big Drum stood with his back against the wall, his instrument ready slung for use.

Opposite him stood Pipes, awaiting the signal to begin his dulcet notes.

Long Bob and Jack, both arrayed in tights, were in the corner doing the " pyra-mid," and laughing heartily at the mishaps that attended the mastery of this difficult feat.

Big Drum gave an impatient tap upon his namesake, and glancing towards the door, muttered—

"I wish she would come. What can the woman be up to with her ? "

"Curling her teeth," suggested Long Bob, as he turned a somersault, his heels flying past Pipes' nose.

They were waiting for Lily, and when she entered the room a spontaneous burst of pleasant astonishment came from the lips of the company.

The child was dressed in white muslin, the skirts cut short, and the body low ; her tresses were loose, and swept her back. Her sweet face was flushed with the hurry of dressing, and perhaps a consciousness that her appearance had caused this outburst of admiration.

"Stunning ! " Drum shouted.

Pipes gasped out something wildly, and wiped the top of his instrument with his dirty fingers.

Long Bob said—

"My eye ! Talk about a fairy, eh, Jack ? "

Jack was silent. The appearance of the lovely child caused his heart to throb quickly, and obeying an uncontrollable im-pulse he ran forward and clasped her in his arms.

"Lily," he said, kissing her white fore-head, "you do look pretty."

She blushed and gently disengaged herself from his embrace, as Big Drum flourished the drum-sticks about.

"Take your places all. Now, Pipes, tune up. Say when you are ready."

Pipes ran up the scale, then finished with a wheezing bass note, and said—

"Ready, Drum."

"Now, then," said the manager, " you must suppose these ere walls is the street, and the windows the people. Now, Bob, you first. You come forward and go on the stage, and make a bow ; after that, when me and Pipes plays, you begin to chuck the balls about."

"All right, Drum ! "

"You, Jack, pick up that rope with the lumps on the ends, and swing 'em about just as though you were keeping the crowd back."

Jack reluctantly left Lily's side, and did as he was directed.

"Stand back, Pipes ; there ain't much of yer, but you is in the way."

Pipes flattened himself against the wall, and Big Drum continued—

"All ready—go on, shadder!"

In a plaintive manner Pipes began, "Why did my master sell me?" and Drum gave the necessary vigour to the air by a plentiful application of the drum-sticks.

Long Bob acquitted himself better than could have been expected, considering the short experience he had had of the profession.

The balls, the hoops, the dagger, and the rings were tried, and at a signal from Big Drum, Pipes left off swinging his head to and fro.

"Now," Drum said, "you must talk all the time you are taking the paper shreds out of the box, but you needn't eat the shreds to-day, 'cos we ain't got too many of 'em ; only go through the motion."

"All right! What am I to say?"

"Anything you likes ; something to make 'em laugh, 'cos the more they laughs the more they'll dub up."

"All right! Something like this." Bob went through the motion of taking a handful of shavings from the box, and cramming them down his throat, pausing every now and then, as he said—"There was only two men, ladies and gentlemen, that ever lived after doing this trick ; they died, you see, from the effects of eating so much paper. All the thin ends gets round their hearts, and they couldn't breathe. Horful, warn't it?"

In taking a fresh mouthful, he went on—"Of course, you have all got eyes, and those eyes were given you to see with ; you then see this is paper, and you must know that if I eat all this I shall die too. Ladies and gentlemen, I don't want to die, so I only chew the paper, but as I shouldn't like to show you the paper in that state, I will bring forth a pole out of my mouth, and the more coppers you drop into the cap the larger the pole will be. Go round with the cap, Jack. Give that gentleman change of a fourpenny-piece ; he wants to give something, and I'm afraid he is too shy to ask for change. Will that do, Drum?"

"Fine, go on."

"Drop 'em in, ladies and gentlemen, drop 'em in, you haven't seen such a company before in the streets ever since you were born. There is no deception—everything is fair and square, and all we ask is a little encouragement. Go on, music!"

This was the signal for Big Drum and Pipes to commence, and while they filled the air with discord, Long Bob slowly drew out the paper pole.

He was seconded by Jack, whose elegant figure and well-shaped limbs added greatly to the effect of his performance.

He was accompanied by spirited music from the conductor, and when he concluded Lily came forward.

The child was a little timid when she began, but under the influence of Jack's encouraging voice, and the shrill notes from Pipes' "torture," she became more at ease ; her tiny feet, encased in red shoes, moved with wondrous rapidity, and when she turned and curtsied gracefully to the admiring audience, Drum declared she would make their "fortins."

Pipes took his instrument from his mouth, and whispered to himself—

"I wish Bob would borrow a shilling, I'm awfully dry."

So ended the rehearsal, and the company looked forward to the morrow with hopeful hearts.

CHAPTER XI.

BIG DRUM AND PIPES BEGIN THEIR NEW ENTERTAINMENT.

AN eminent public orator was wont to recite his maiden speech in a field of cabbages ; he compared them to a large audience, and, after a few discourses, mustered sufficient courage to appear before a crowded assembly.

He found a vast difference between the sea of faces that were upturned towards him and the cabbages, and he became so nervous that he was unable to proceed beyond the third sentence, and, overwhelmed with shame and confusion, retired.

A friend asked the young orator why he had been compelled to make such an undignified retreat, and received for an answer—

"I have been in the habit of comparing an audience to a field of cabbages ; but when brought before the many faces and restless eyes, I found them very different to my quiet listeners. I did not care for the faces, it was the eyes that did for me."

Big Drum's company must have experienced some such sensation when they made their *début* after the rehearsal. When performing to the bare walls the matter was easy ; but when the "pitch" was made, and Long Bob stepped to the centre and began to throw the balls, his nerves became unsteady, and to make matters worse, one of the balls, in place of dropping on his hand, fell upon his upturned face, striking him between the eyes, and, as Bob afterwards expressed it—

"I saw all the lamps lighted up and dancing before me."

The first "pitch" was a failure, in spite of the energetic music of Big Drum and Pipes, and when the crowd began to laugh and a number of the boys to cast ridicule upon the performance, Drum threw his instrument on his back and started off in high dudgeon.

The second "pitch" was no better. Long Bob had not yet recovered from the blow he had received, and when he had the balls well in play he sprang backwards to escape a second blow.

The consequence was a shout of laughter from the bystanders, and again they were compelled to pack up and depart.

R. J. was considerably chapfallen by this second failure, and as they moved briskly through the streets he mentally debated a sudden dive down an unfrequented street, and a return to his late master.

He would have done so but for his affection for Jack and Lily.

"No!" so ran his thoughts. "I'll try again, and if the balls all come in my face, and break my snout, I'll stick to 'em until I can do it to rights."

Pipes stayed behind his brother musician until Long Bob came up to him. When they were walking abreast he bowed his head and whispered—

"Shut your eyes next time. It's the people that does it."

"Right, Pipes." was the reply. "It's their eyes that makes me nervous ; I can't stand 'em. But I will try your dodge next time."

"Do, Bob, or else we shan't get a blessed penny, and there ain't a morsel of anything to eat when we gets home."

"All right, old 'un," Long Bob answered. "I'll do it next 'pitch' we make. You see if I don't."

"Hopes you will, Bob—hopes you will."

Pipes whispered this, then hurried after Big Drum, who, driven to desperation, was looking out for a favourable spot to make the third, and, if successful, the last "pitch."

Jack Lennox and Lily were walking side by side, both somewhat timid as to the result of their first essay before the public, yet anxious that Long Bob should finish his share of the performance with more credit than he had hitherto done.

"It is very unfortunate, Lil," said Jack Lennox, "that poor Bob should make such a mess of the business. I wonder how we shall manage when our turn comes ? "

"I hope better than he has," she said ; "yet I am afraid not."

"Why so, Lil ? "

"I feel so frightened," she said, "when I think of having to dance in the midst of a crowd, and the boys making all sorts of rude remarks."

Jack's face reddened.

"They had better not," he said, fiercely, "say anything to you ; if they do I will make them remember it."

"You mustn't take any notice, Jack ; for, as Pipes told me, public performers are obliged to put up with a great many insults without taking the least notice."

"They may do so, I shall not."

Long Bob joined them at this moment.

His face expressed the misery he felt at his non-success, and as he sidled beside Jack, he said—

"Well, Jack, what do you think of this muff, eh ? I ought to be kicked for being a fool."

"You will get on all right next time, Bob."

"I'm afraid not, Jack ; I dare say I could manage it if the people wouldn't stare at me so."

"Did the ball hurt you when it came on your face ?" Lily asked ; "it sounded as if it did."

Long Bob rubbed the tender spot, as he answered—

"Hurt me ? I should say it did. I didn't know for a minute whether my eyes were knocked out or not, but," he added, half savagely, "the pain I felt when the ball fell was nothing to the back-ache this beastly thing gives me."

He gave the dancing-board anything but a friendly look as he spoke. Long Bob little knew, when he borrowed the heavy kitchen shutter from Mrs. Smith, that it would fall to his lot to carry it about the street.

"Let me help you," Jack said ; "I am not tired."

"No," said Long Bob ; "I'll stick to it. It's a punishment for being such a muff as I have been."

They were passing down a wide street when this conversation took place, and much to Bob's relief, Big Drum halted at the corner of a bye-turning, and placed the strap of his instrument around the back of his neck.

"A pitch," Bob said, advancing boldly to the centre of the road ; "keep your eye on me, Jack ; I'm going in for a win this time."

Jack nodded encouragingly, and Pipes, as Bob placed the half shutter on the road, whispered—

"Think of the coin, Bob. Not a farthing amongst us, and nothing to eat all day. Shut your eyes, and go in."

"All right, old 'un ; play up."

Big Drum eyed Bob savagely as he began to unpack the conjuring implements, and his face became ruddier than ever when Pipes began the music without the signal from the drum.

"Can't you wait?" he said, fiercely. "That squeaking noise will frighten the people away. They don't come to have the stummick-ache."

Pipes became silent, and reflectively rubbed the end of his scarf across his nose.

"He allus pitches on me," thought Pipes; "if I hadn't have given that first bar of the polka the people wouldn't have stopped."

Long Bob had by this time made his preparations, and with an amount of courage which startled Big Drum, and caused him to strike a false note, R. J. threw one of the gilt balls above his head, and called out—

"Now then, music! Don't you see the ladies and gentlemen awaiting to behold the Chinese juggler beat into nothing?"

The music began in earnest; so did Long Bob's performance, for, to the surprise of the company in general and the performer himself, Bob kept the three balls in motion.

He had gone in to win, and kept his word. After the first few seconds he forgot the crowd which had by this time gathered, and went through the part assigned him even better than at the rehearsal.

Big Drum was in ecstacies, and the parchment suffered; so did the organs of hearing possessed by the bystanders.

The unexpected sight had a far different effect upon Pipes; it took his breath away, and though his head moved from side to side his instrument was silent.

This fact was unnoticed by all save Jack and Lily, and as she stood with her hands crossed upon the brave boy's shoulder, she whispered—

"Pipes is not playing a note."

"Never mind," Jack answered; "Drum is making up for it. What are those boys laughing at opposite us?"

"At Bob, I think; his tongue is hanging out of his mouth, and makes him look so—"

She paused abruptly, and looked up as a hand was lightly placed upon her shoulder.

Jack's eyes followed her upturned face, and to his surprise he beheld Monsieur Jules Latour standing behind them. Earl Falconmere's ex-valet had not time to learn whether it was the young girl he had known under such different circumstances, for Long Bob finished the pole business just as Latour was about to speak.

"It is our turn, Lil," said the boy, drawing her quickly away; then as they took their places upon the board he whispered—

"Did you see the Frenchman?"

"I did," she answered; "he seemed as though he wished to speak to me. What does he want with me, I wonder?"

"No good," replied Jack; "he has rogue written on his forehead. We had better not know him, Lil; if he speaks to us I will answer."

During the time these words were exchanged, the children were dancing opposite each other, and Monsieur Jules—a cunning smile upon his face—stood well forward, keenly watching them.

He was not certain yet of their identity, and to obtain a closer view he came within the circle, and received more than he wished.

Long Bob had taken the cord used to keep the crowd back from Jack, and, being elated with his success, began to twirl the ends over his head.

Whether by accident or design, one of the stuffed ends came plump in the face of Monsieur Jules, and filled his eyes with sharp gritty dust.

He stepped smartly back amid a shout of laughter from the crowd, the juvenile members of which began a series of remarks which added to Monsieur Jules's discomfort and anger.

Many wished to know the tradesman's name that manufactured the ex-valet's glossy hat; others made rude inquiries respecting the amount of stiffening used in the preparation of his collar.

Monsieur Latour likened the boys to pigs; but as he made the remark in his own language they knew not the meaning of his savage mutterings, and he was allowed to pass through them without a shower of nice thin, round stones, which the London street boy knows so well how to use.

The painful sensation increasing every moment in his eyes, Latour went inside a chemist's shop which stood near, and by the time the bathing business was over the street performers had disappeared.

The pitch had been as successful as could be expected, each of the performers affirming that Lily's graceful dancing had been the cause of the large receipts, which Pipes, as treasurer, carried in a small square box.

There was no doubt that Long Bob's misadventure with the Frenchman put the crowd in good humour, and caused them to part with the coin with more freedom than they would otherwise have done; at least, this holds good with a portion of the audience.

The remainder—and these were the most respectable—were charmed with the little girl and her partner's dancing. Perhaps their tender years and remarkable beauty had also a share in thus filling the exchequer.

It was a picture an artist would have been proud to have represented when Jack and Lily stood face to face on the board.

The girl's red shoes and flesh-coloured hose contrasted prettily with her snow-white spangle-bound skirt, and her long light tresses, floating like a golden mist, and her strikingly lovely face and white shoulders, brought to the imagination of the beholders the nymphs one sometimes meets in the works of the old masters.

In her dancing she kept time with the somewhat rough accompaniment which Big Drum dignified by the name of music, and often the orchestra, instead of playing for her to dance by their time, found themselves following the movements of her twinkling tiny feet.

There was a sunny look upon her face as she held the handsome boy's hand—a look that deepened into a rosy blush when he gave her a word of praise or encouragement. Then, at the whispered word—

"Now!"

She released her grasp of his hand, and placing the tips of her fingers together, raised them over her head; then, receding from her partner, she unconsciously assumed the most graceful and charming attitudes.

It was her heart that directed these movements, for whatever posture she assumed her eyes were fixed upon the boy's face, and though every action was in perfect harmony with her graceful form, and at times her head became averted, her depthless blue eyes never wandered from the flushed, happy, boyish face before her.

When they concluded, and the little performers bowed to those who stood around—and they were many, and among them, to judge by external appearances, were a few who were no strangers to the sight of the highly-paid dancers of Her Majesty's Theatre—a murmur of admiration came from their lips, and such exclamations as "Bravo, little ones!—first-rate!—bravo!—bravo!" were heard; and, while Pipes went round with the box, Big Drum vented his joyful feelings on the parchment heads of his high-toned instrument. They gave three performances after this; then, night coming on, and the company being tired, Big Drum proposed a little refreshment before they returned to Mrs. Smith's.

Pipes, as usual, shed tears over a quart of half-and-half, and whispered to himself—

"They says, and I believe 'em, that everything happens for the best. Now, there was the Buffler. He sloped with the funds, and everything he could carry. That was for the best, 'cos we takes these youngsters into the purfession, and they brings in the coin like—like beer goes down Drum's throat," he added, lost for a simile; "yes, like it rolls down Drum's throat, and it does go down, too. Ah! the pot's empty again, and I ain't hardly tasted."

Poor Pipes! He was troubled with a very bad memory, especially where beer-drinking was concerned. To listen to his assertion, he never by any chance more than tasted. Perhaps this was the cause of his unsteady gait when they began their return homeward; or possibly it might have been the performances, which in the three last instances had gone off without the least hitch. Certain it was that he did roll from side to side, and mutter strange things in a thick undertone.

When crossing the well-known turning that leads from New Oxford Street to the Seven Dials, Long Bob came to a dead stop, and placed the heavy shutter on the pavement.

"What's the matter?" Drum asked. "Is it getting heavy?"

"Like lead," was the answer. "I believe the old gal wouldn't have let me have it only she knew I should have enough of the beastly thing the first day."

"You must take it home, Bob."

"I know that, Drum; but I think I could carry it better if I knew it was the last time."

Big Drum looked puzzled, and waved his hand majestically towards a crowd of little boys who closed round him when he came to a standstill.

"This is what I mean," Bob said; "down here there is a old chap as keeps a broker's shop."

"What, Ben Isaacs the Jew?"

"The very identical. You knows him then, Drum?"

"Yes," the manager slowly answered; "we once had a little business together—that is, he did the business, and I didn't want him."

"Grabbed your sticks?"

Big Drum nodded.

"He's good at that," said Long Bob. "I've heard he once took three cracked plates and a kettle from a' old widow, because she couldn't pay her rent, but that ain't it. I've been thinking he might have an old dancing-board that would do better than this."

"So he might," said Drum. "How much could you get it for?"

"Eighteenpence, I should think; anyhow, give us two bob. Pipes can take the shutter till I catch up to you. I shan't be long."

Big Drum gave him the money, and Bob ran off at full speed towards old Ben Isaac's.

When Pipes was told of the treat in store for him, he applied the fringe of his worsted scarf several times to his face, and eyeing the board, woefully remarked—

"I'm the solo reed instrument in the band, and don't carry the properties."

Big Drum waxed very wrath, and seizing Pipes by the collar with one hand, pointed to the board with the other.

"Collar it," he said, "or you don't have a blessed farthing of to-day's coin."

"I shan't touch it, so you needn't bully me."

Jack Lennox overheard the squabble while he was busy threatening to punch a juvenile butcher's nose.

He parted Big Drum and Pipes, then trying to lift the shutter, said—

"Don't grumble about it, I will take it home."

"You shan't," Pipes said, leaning forward and taking it from the boy; "I'll take it home for you, Jack, but to-morrow I cuts the concern; then," as he raised the board to his shoulder, "we'll see how you get on without proper music."

"Better without you," said Drum. "I hope you will go; you've been long enough living on the fat of the land for nothing; for I calls whistling on that thing nothing."

"Quite enough, Drum," said the injured Pipes; "remember to-morrow."

"I'll make you remember to-night," growled Drum, as he followed his companions, "if you don't mind."

They were soon overtaken by Long Bob. He had purchased the article required, and left it until the next day in old Ben's care.

He relieved Pipes of his burden, and much happier than when they started, they reached the dingy third floor back.

Mrs. Smith saw by their faces that fortune had been kind, and with a gushing generosity that made Long Bob wince, she offered them the loan of the shutter while they honoured her house with their presence.

"Thank'ee, ma'am," the long youth said, as he carried the Nemesis to the subterranean chamber to which it belonged, "we are much obliged; but Drum and myself thinks it would be imposing on your good nature to take it again."

"Oh dear, no, not at all; you are quite welcome to it—quite."

"We know that, ma'am, that's the very reason we won't borrow; you see the stones may do it a lot of harm, and that would not be right."

Mrs. Smith still protested her perfect willingness to lend the article, and Long Bob in like manner declined. When she was enabled to begin the ascent of the narrow stairs, Mrs. Smith, had she followed him, would have overheard him mutter—

"The old gal is too kind—her kindness is quite overpowering, at least it has been to me to-day. Carry that again! no, not if it was made of gold."

When he entered the third floor back he found Big Drum and Pipes, and the two children, seated at the little table; the latter, he saw, were trying to abstain from laughing, and by Drum's serious face he guessed that something was wrong.

The box Pipes had carried was open, and the contents, quite a little heap, were piled before the manager, who commented thus—

"You see, that makes eleven shillings and fourpence ha'penny; the bad penny and ha'penny would have made eleven and a tanner. Now look here, the first thing is to divide it among us, and as Pipes is a going to leave us to-morrow, he shall have his share now."

Pipes looked repentant, but made no remark.

"Now," Drum continued, "we must give five bob to the chandler's shop, five to Mrs. Smith; that's ten, isn't it, Jack?"

"Ten shillings down—balance, one shilling and fourpence ha'penny."

Pipes rubbed his nose with his finger. The fifth share, he thought, was not much to retire with.

"One and fourpence ha'penny," said Drum, "to be divided. Let's see, how it is to be done fairly?"

"Let's go five out of nine for the lot," suggested Long Bob.

"Young man," Drum said, "gambling ain't allowed in the company; remember you are a purfessionel, and purfessionels are respectable."

Bob screwed up his comical face behind the sage speaker, and caused Jack and Lily to burst into a fit of laughter.

Big Drum looked fiercely towards Pipes, but as that passive gentleman was studying a small hole in the ceiling, the look did not take the desired effect.

"One shilling and fourpence ha'penny," said Drum, pushing his white hat aside, and burying his fingers in his unkempt hair. "I'm blest if I knows how to do it."

"Give it to me," said the incorrigible Bob; "I'll spend it in ribbons for Lily."

"Young man," Drum said, severely, "this ain't a time for buffoolery——"

"Buffoonery, Drum," little Jack said, and Drum became red to the roots of his hair.

"Ah, so it is," he said, looking round to ascertain whether there was a possibility of having a row with Pipes. The latter was too quick. When Drum turned his head, the melancholy one was silently studying a faded rose upon the paper on the wall. "Yes, now I remember, you are right, Jack."

He paused for a few seconds, and looked from the little pile of coppers set aside for distribution to Pipes's face, but failed to catch the solo instrumentalist's eye.

"The only way," he said, "at least, as I can see, to do it, will be to have threepence each all round; that will be one shilling and threepence, and——"

"I'll go you first time," Bob jerked out, "for the three ha'pence."

Big Drum pretended not to hear this.

"The odd three ha'pence I propose we gives to Pipes, to help him on the road. Here you are, shadder; fourpence ha'penny. Count it."

Pipes squinted down at the magnificent sum, and possibly dazzled by its magnitude, he closed his eyes, and whispered—

"Don't want it."

Big Drum repeated the words.

"No," Pipes said, "I don't."

"Take it, old 'un," Bob said; "it will help you on the road. Eh! What are you shaking your head for?"

"I ain't going on the road," came in a faint whisper, "so I shan't want it."

"Where are you going, then, old 'un?"

"To a place," whispered Pipes, "where they don't want any money, and where I shan't be in anybody's way; that's where I'm going (sob), and the sooner I goes the better."

Both ends of the dirty scarf were crowded in Pipes' eyes, as he gave vent to a flow of tears at the conclusion of these pathetic words.

Big Drum was much affected.

He rubbed his nose with the back of his right hand, then mechanically rubbed the right palm with the back of his left; he was not aware that the right hand was already before his nose when he brought up the left.

He watched Pipes for a few seconds, then, unable to bear the sight any longer, jumped to his feet, and pulling the rusty scarf from his thin companion's eyes, blustered out—

"You ain't a going to drownd yourself, Pipes?"

"I (sob)—I is."

"Don't," said Drum; "I didn't mean to offend you, Pipes; let's be friends again, and I'll stand two pots of cooper."

Pipes unclosed one eye, and whispered—

"You can't, you've only got fourpence."

Long Bob burst into a roar of laughter, then stood on his head in the centre of the room.

Lily and Jack joined in the laugh—the drollery of Pipes' remark was more than they could possibly endure.

"No more I ain't," said Drum, "but I can borrow some, so don't drownd yourself, Pipes."

Pipes consented not to rob the musical world of his power after a proper amount of persuasion had been used, and by the time Long Bob—who volunteered to go for the beer—returned, the manager and the solo performer were good friends again.

"Now, you young uns," Big Drum said, "me and Pipes has been talking matters over, and we thinks the odd one and four and a half had better be spent in grub, so that we shan't go on tick any more at the chandler's shop; what do you say?"

"Motion carried," cried Long Bob; "and the chairman to be bonneted."

Big Drum knew sufficient of his volatile young friend to cause him to take off his dirty white hat and place it beneath the table. He feared the bonneting would be carried out, and had too much affection for his valuable hat to risk it being damaged.

"Just as you like," Jack said; "I and Lily are agreeable."

"Very well," said Drum. "Now, young man, go and lay this out to the best advantage, and remember you are a purfessionel, and purfessionels never picks the corners off the loaf."

"All right, old Gooseberry; hand over the filthy lucre."

"Ochre!" Drum said. "What is that?"

"The coin. Ha! ha! ha!"

"Never heard it called ochre afore," said Drum. "Ochre; what a name!"

"Do you know," Bob said, "what the immortal Shakespeare said about a name?"

"I don't; but Pipes ought to. He once performed in 'Hamlet.'"

"Did he?" said Bob, doubtfully. "Well, he'll know this is what he says. Listen. *A name would smell just as sweet if it was a rose.* There, Drum; there's poetry for you."

Saying this Bob disappeared through the door to return in ten minutes with the produce of the one four and a half.

"Block ornaments," he began, "sixpence; loaf fourpence, that's ten; quarter of cheese twopence, that's twelve; candle a penny, that's thirteen; matches a ha'penny, thirteen and a half; tossed the tatur-man and lost, that's fourteen and a half."

The "block ornaments," as Bob termed them, were stale scraps of meat purchased at the butcher's; but uninviting as they looked, the company were so little accustomed to such food that they beheld in the "ornaments" a foretaste of quite a luxurious repast.

They were without a fire, so our long friend went to Mrs. Smith, one hand carrying the paper which held the meat, the other holding the five shillings on account as a peace-offering to that most estimable lady of the very uncommon name.

With her sweetest smile she relieved him of the money, and grimly gave him permission to use the gridiron whenever he liked.

While Bob was thus engaged, Big Drum made known a project he had formed during their homeward walk, and strange to say, although both the children hailed it with delight, Pipes raised a loud dissentient whisper against it.

"I've been thinking, my dears," Drum said, "that as next Monday is the fust of

May, it would not be a bad dodge to start a Jack-in-the-green; there's just enough to do the business comfortable. I'll do the music; you, Lily, shall be the lady, and go round with a brass ladle; you, Jack, shall be the gentleman, and wear a cocked hat; Bob will do very well for a clown, and if I do the music, which I shall, Pipes can be—"

"All hot, all hot!" cried Long Bob, rushing into the room with a plate of cooked block ornaments.

"What am I to be?" Pipes asked, wiping his mouth with the fringe. "You didn't finish your speech, Drum. What am I to be?"

"You," Drum said; "why, Jack-in-the-green, of course."

Pipes gave a groan and turned his eyes upwards. He was quite overcome by this announcement.

CHAPTER XII.
JACK LENNOX BECOMES AN OBJECT OF INTEREST.

As the ivy clings to the fallen masonry of an old tower, so Simon Redley clung to the blackened remains of Falconmere Abbey.

He was the forest-keeper, and had grown gray in the service of the noble family which, by the earl's supposed death, had become extinct.

He had begun by serving the earl's father, and like a retainer of old he felt proud of the family, and would have resented an insult levelled at the lord of the good old place with a fierceness that smacked strongly of the good old feudal days.

Like snow melting beneath the sunlight, the crowd of domestics had left the charred and massive ruins—all had gone save Simon Redley, and he, with his gray hairs bowed low, sat at the open door of his cottage, looking sadly at the desolation which marked the progress of the fierce destroying element.

The morning was young—the orb of day just tingeing the dew-covered grass and dank foliage of the trees—yet, at this early hour, the old forest-keeper was astir, and engaged in the work he had begun since Falconmere's earl perished amid the fallen walls of his palatial home.

He was looking for the remains of the proud, stern man amid the ruins, working alone, his only aid a small crowbar, by which he removed various heavy masses of the strange-looking heap.

The forest-keeper had stood by when the search was made for the earl's body, and though not a trace was found, he clung to a belief which had crept to his heart, and caused him to work in the endeavour to learn its truth or falsity.

"He must be there," he muttered, as he paused in his work; "yes, there amongst those girders and heavy stones. Such is not a fit resting-place for the last of an old and noble family."

He plied his crowbar again, and became so engaged that he did not notice a tall, bronzed, military-looking man, who crossed the keep and passed within a few feet of the forest-keeper.

He knew not of the stranger's presence until a deep and somewhat subdued voice said, in hushed accents—

"There has been foul work here, Simon."

The old man looked up. The stranger's voice awoke a dim recollection in the keeper's mind, and passing his hand over his brow, he gazed at the calm, handsome, passionless face.

"Ay," he said; "may the hand wither that fired the old Abbey! May Heaven's curse blight those who did the fell deed!"

He continued to gaze searchingly at the stranger, and as though a flash of light suddenly passed through his brain, he dropped the crowbar and exclaimed—

"It is Lady Alicia's husband!"

"Yes, Simon," was the answer, and the stranger grasped the old man's hand; "years, I find, have not effaced my form from your remembrance."

"I never forget," Simon Redley said; "you above all I should remember."

"Sixteen years," said the stranger, "must have altered me much; it is a long time, Simon."

"It is; but I should have known you had it been sixty. It were impossible to forget the handsome boy who had so oft been my companion in happier times than this. So, Master Walter, you have returned, and she who should have been here to welcome you, has long since gone to the tomb."

The stranger sighed deeply, and a gleam of passion was visible in his dark eye.

"Yes, Simon," he said, "I am alone in the world; my wife dead, and my children"—here his voice faltered—"God knows where they are."

"Children!" repeated Simon—"children! There was a rumour—a strange one it was—that she came here to die; but I heard not the least mention of a child."

"There were two," said the stranger, sadly. "Tidings of one I have gleaned, but the other—so like her fair, beautiful mother—has gone, none know whither!"

The forest-keeper looked straight into the stricken man's face, and said—

"Your words are strange, Master Walter —you are Master Walter to me, though you have changed since we last met."

"Much changed, Simon."

"Ay," the old man said, as though speaking to himself, "he is ; but children ! It is the first I have heard that my lord's daughter was a mother, for they placed her in the vault, and her own name, not his, was upon the coffin."

"That coffin," said Walter Carlin, did not contain the body of Lady Alicia."

Simon Redley started.

"She did not die," Walter continued, "until ten years after that mock funeral took place."

"Master Walter," said the forest-keeper, "are you speaking the truth ? "

"As I hope for mercy," he said, "I am."

The old man stepped close beside the speaker, and pointing to the cottage, said—

"Let us go inside ; we can talk better there. Oh, God, that I should have lived to have raised my hand against his child ! "

They went to the keeper's lodge, then the old man told the story of a report that a child belonging to the earl's daughter was among the gipsies. He told how the story had been discredited by the earl and his servants, and how the former had given the keepers orders to drive the gipsies from the place.

"I obeyed those orders," said Simon, regretfully, "and my hand was ever the first to strike the vagrants. One day, when I went my rounds of the park, I found a portion of the fence had been broken down, and soon after this discovery I saw a beggar urchin chasing a butterfly ; the little fellow showed no signs of fear at my approach, and as I raised my whip to lash him from the grounds, he looked me full in the face and dared me to strike him."

The forest-keeper paused, and the stranger, who drank in every word with an eagerness that bespoke more than ordinary interest, compressed his lips, and as an angry spot reddened his cheeks, he bent forward and fixed his dark eyes upon the forest-keeper's face.

"I could not," Simon resumed, "carry out my intention—God be praised I did not—for as the sunlight streamed upon the lad's face I beheld the exact counterpart of your features."

Captain Carlin sprang from his seat and hastily asked—

"When did this occur ? "

"Not a month since," Simon answered ; "and from that hour to this my mind has been tormented trying to satisfy itself as to the truth of those reports which were so rife some ten years since."

"Simon," said his visitor, his twitching lips belying the outward calmness he assumed, "that boy was my son."

"I knew it, Master Walter, my heart told me so ; yet—fool—dolt I was not to act upon the dictates of my heart and take the boy under my care! I knew you would come, Master Walter, and it would have been a joyful hour for me to have given your beautiful boy to your arms."

A sigh came from the sorrowing father's lips, and he bowed his head in lowly submission to the great sorrow which had fallen so heavily upon him.

"He may be found," Simon said, in a voice so low that it scarcely broke the stillness; "there is hope, Master Walter. The newspapers and the police may do much for you, for there must be many who have seen the children since they left Falconmere.

"The child, is he not with the gipsies ?"

"No, Master Walter. The tribe carried off a little girl that my lord loved as purely as though she had come from the old stock ; they took her away in revenge for the earl appearing against one of their tribe who had broken into my lord's chamber."

"But the boy, what had he to do with the child's abduction ?"

"They were playmates, Master Walter. The little girl, shut up in the great Abbey, and never suffered to go beyond the grounds, found a companion in the ragged boy, who, in defiance of my men, would climb the fences to meet the fair child. I have seen them together, Master Walter, and never before have my eyes rested upon two beings more gifted with outward beauty."

The stranger was now sitting with folded arms ; his face turned towards Simon, and every faculty absorbed by the old man's words.

"When the tribe took her away," Simon continued, "the boy escaped with her from the camp. He showed the better blood that ran in his veins by the chivalrous manner in which he defended her from an attempt made by one of the tribe to recapture them. He fired upon the fellow, and shattered his leg."

The officer's face wore an expression of pride. He was a soldier, and the use Jack had made of the gun was sufficient to fill his heart with pride, and added to the yearning he felt to discover his noble boy.

He made a gesture for the old man to proceed.

"He left the gipsy prone by the roadside," resumed Simon, "and came to the Abbey—alas ! it was to behold the grand old place in flames, and Lily's benefactor consumed by the raging fire. They must have been startled by the appearance of some of the tribe, for from that moment to this no trace has been found of them."

"Was there a search ?"

"Ay, Master Walter ; the tribe, baulked of their prey, were like bloodhounds upon the children's trail. They found out that the young pair had passed through Mayburg

AT THE MERCY OF TINKER TOM.

hand-in-hand, but after that they were at fault. The boy must have profited by the cunning the gipsies had taught him, to escape thus successfully."

"Thank heaven they have! for the passions of those lawless outcasts once aroused, they would destroy the boy to satiate their revenge."

"They're a bad lot, Master Walter, and I hope that one who has cause to hunt the children down may never behold them again."

"Of whom do you speak, Simon?"

The captain's face was anxious—the danger to his boy which Simon's words foreshadowed for a moment caused a thrill to pass through his frame.

"I speak of the man whose leg was shattered by the boy—a powerful, ill-looking ruffian who used to prowl about here while the smoke yet rose from the ruins—he will keep his word, Master Walter, should he once discover them."

"He had better never have been born," said the soldier, firmly; "if he harm my boy, not the united power of his tribe would save him from my hand."

"It was but yesterday," Simon said, "that he was able to start upon their trail, for in the early morn he stood among those trees, looking with such devilish triumph upon the fell event, that twice I had my gun raised to fire; but the thought of the boy's safety came to my mind, and I approached him as a friend, and learnt from his lips all I have told you."

"You acted wisely, Simon."

"So far, Master Walter, but I have thought since that there would have been less danger to the boy had I disabled the ruffian."

"It would have been useless—others of the band would have taken up the pursuit."

"Perhaps so, sir."

Captain Carlin took a small book from his breast pocket, and opening it, said—

"Give me some information respecting this gipsy's appearance that I may know him when we meet?"

Simon described Tinker Tom so accurately that his recognition would be easy.

"He limps," Simon said in conclusion, "for the wound is not yet healed, and nothing but the fierce passion for revenge could enable him to endure the pain he suffers."

"I shall recognize him," said the officer, closing his book, "by this description; it will point out my boy's foe."

"Master Walter," said the old keeper, rising, "I need not ask the question; you are going in search of your boy."

"I am, and until he is found shall know no rest, either of mind or body."

"If," Simon said, "an old man's assistance is of any service to you, I will go with you;

for should the ruffian offer a determined resistance it will require a strong hand to obtain his release."

"No, Simon, I shall be better alone upon my errand. We shall meet again. Should I find my noble boy——"

"If you do not?"

"I shall find him, Simon, though the search may be long and full of peril. My heart tells me all will yet be well."

"Pray heaven your words may be prophetic!"

The soldier rose and moved towards the door, and Simon, as they walked slowly from the house, said—

"You will be kind to the little girl, Master Walter, when you meet them. Think not of the wrong the man who loved her has done you, but let the fulfilment of the solemn duty you are about to go upon make you——"

Captain Carlin stayed Simon by a gentle gesture of his hand.

"I needed not this from you," the officer said. "I shall be kind to the girl, if, with Heaven's help, I find them. But tell me, Simon, what child is this that so won the heart of that stern, terrible man?"

"She was taken to the Abbey by the late earl, sir, and, as far as I can learn, he first met her in the company of two tramps, a man and woman; the child was being beaten by the woman, and her screams for mercy and the manner in which she called for her mamma caused the earl to interfere. I believe the pair of wretches were only too glad to escape by giving up the child, for he—and you know, Master Walter, how terrible he was in his anger—accused them of having stolen the child—an accusation which was, upon questioning the child, found to be correct."

"Is this all you know about the child?"

"It is, sir."

They soon after parted; the sorrowing father upon his mission, and old Simon, the forest keeper, to return to the mound of fallen masonry, there to search for the buried remains of his late lord.

Pursuing his way to the little village of Maybury, the soldier pondered over the strange story of the meeting between the earl and Lily.

"If," he thought, "Simon Redley's account of the meeting was true, there must have been a great change in Earl Herbert since my poor Alicia was thrust from the Abbey gates, and in her utter hopelessness sought a Lethe for her sorrows in the dark waters of the pool."

It was night before he reached the village, and entering the little hostel, he inquired for the landlord.

Boniface came; the advent of such a distinguished-looking customer was not in the daily course of events.

Could he be accommodated for the night?

The landlord said he could—he had a chamber which was fit for a nobleman. Mine host believed this himself, so little wonder that he endeavoured to imbue others with his belief.

"Refreshment, sir? yes—what would you like? We have eggs, sir, eggs poached and fried bacon; some of the finest you have ever eaten—my own curing, sir."

"Anything else?"

"Yes," said mine host, looking through the window at a venerable old fowl, who had gone to roost upon the lower branch of the tree on which was nailed the sign-board, "we have fowls, sir; but I am almost afraid we can't catch any to-night—they are such cunning beggars, sir, and always hide when they see a customer approach."

"Never mind, poach me a few eggs."

"Yes, sir."

The landlord left the room, delighted—he had again saved the life of the solitary old Spanish hen, without the character of his house suffering.

Boniface wished his visitors to understand that his poultry-yard was unlimited, and with the old fowl's assistance he managed to carry out the delusion.

"Wonder who he is?" said mine host to his wife; "he seems a gentleman."

The dame paused in the act of breaking the third egg, and answered—

"You said the same when that there Frenchman came here, upsetting the place with his airs and graces."

"True, Margery, true; but you must confess that I am not often mistaken."

Margery would not confess to her husband's perceptive powers, but, with wife-like contradiction, refuted his words by bringing forward many instances wherein he had signally failed in his judgment.

To mine host's relief the bell rang, and he escaped the lecture he had so unwittingly brought upon his head.

"Yours is a very quiet little place," the stranger said, when Boniface entered the room.

"Yes, sir. We don't have much noise here when it's not hirings, and the like."

"Very few travellers pass through, I should imagine?"

"Not many, sir, since the Maybury station opened; though, after all, it isn't Maybury, for the place is a long way from here; and then, again, we don't have more than two trains a day stop. If it wasn't for the young gents as comes here to fish, I don't know what we should do, for, you see, sir, we are a poor lot in the village."

The stranger fell into the host's humour by telling him he thought so from the observations he had made when passing through.

"Ah!" the landlord said, "times are not as they were before the railroad came."

"I suppose not."

"Then, sir, we used to count upon two grand nights a week. That was when the commercial travellers came through on their way to Dover; but now the sight of a strange face is sufficient to talk about for a week after."

"If they have passed through here," thought the captain, "I may yet be able to overtake them."

"Talking of strange faces," the landlord continued, "a queer thing happened this last week."

"Indeed!" remarked the traveller, startled, he knew not why, by the landlord's words.

"The fact of it was, two children came through the village, and after just staying here to get a drink of water and a mouthful of bread and cheese, which the missus gave them, they went on right out in the open country, and, from what I could see of it, they were in a most awful fright——"

"John, John!"

"That's the missus," said the landlord, turning his head in the direction of the shrill voice, "and the supper is ready."

He hurried from the room, leaving his visitor's mind a prey to the most intense anguish. He would have called the man back, but fearful that his anxiety would be the cause of stopping any further conversation, he sat, silently watching and waiting for the landlord's return.

He repeated his host's words over many times. They were frightened—what was to follow? Had they been overtaken and brought back to the inn by the ruffianly gipsy; if so, what had become of them since?"

The feeling he experienced when mine host returned with the tray was as though a heavy, cold hand had released its hold from his heart.

"Supper, sir, and done to a turn; what time would you like to retire?"

With a forced calmness the sad-hearted man pointed to a chair, and said—

"Be seated, landlord; you have strangely excited my curiosity respecting the cause of the children's fear."

"Oh!" exclaimed mine host, as though astonished that his words had made any impression on the stranger's mind, "but the eggs are getting cold."

Walter Carlin pushed the tray from him as he said—

"Finish your story, landlord; I cannot rest until my curiosity is satisfied."

Mine host's face was expressive of much surprise as he resumed—

"They had not much to fear after all, sir."

The listener breathed with more freedom

"For no one came after them until the next day, then a tall thin foreigner came post-haste through the village, and made all sorts of inquiries about the boy—he didn't care much for the girl ; he said it was the boy he wanted."

"Did he overtake them?"

"I don't think he did, sir ; for you see, as they took to the open country, and our place being, as it were, right in the centre of the cross-roads, why, they ought to have come on the Gorton Road ; then again, by crossing a field, they would have come on the London Road—so you see, sir, it just depends which way they turned."

"Exactly—I feared that the man's chance was but a small one."

"His was, sir—but the next day another came—on the same errand—a rough, savage-looking gipsy fellow—he wanted them both—and when he turned from the door, I told him he ought not to walk with such a leg as he had—why he could hardly crawl."

"Well, well, what answer did he make?"

"Such a one, sir, as made my blood run cold : ' My leg will be all right when I find the young cub and the girl.' It wasn't his words so much, as the way he showed his teeth."

Hurriedly bringing his recital to an end, he raised the cover from the dish of eggs, and, making a profound bow, left the room.

CHAPTER XIII.

A STREET TRANSFORMATION SCENE.

THE amazement depicted on Pipes' face when Big Drum announced the honour in store for him was exquisitely ludicrous, and caused the children to burst into a hearty fit of laughter.

"It ain't a bit o' use, Pipes," Drum said, "for you to turn up your eyes and make ugly faces, 'cos you'll have to do it."

"But," said Pipes, appealingly, "I don't know nothing about the business, and you do ; why don't you do the part?"

He shifted out of Big Drum's reach, and held up the ragged end of his scarf as a protecting shield, at the end of his speech.

"Me do Jack-in-the-green!" said Big Drum ; "me! you must be mad, Pipes ; who's to see to the music?"

"That's easy enough," said Pipes ; "I can take the drum for once."

Drum looked the disgust he felt. "You!" he said, "why, if a puff of wind was to come round the corner and catch the head of the drum, you'd be blown away."

Pipes swallowed this allusion to his spare figure, and whispered—

"You can't do both instruments anyhow, and yours by itself won't do."

"It would do at a pinch," Big Drum said,

"'cos it would draw ; but as you is to be Jack-in-the-green, I'll take the two."

Pipes groaned dismally, and whispered to himself—

"He'll spoil my instrument ; that's what will happen."

"It's all cut and dried now," Big Drum said, "so we'll have the banquet, then go on again arterwards."

Pipes, overcome by the fall from solo instrumentalist to the part assigned him by Big Drum, had but little appetite for the repast, until Long Bob, who was plying his knife and fork with an energy quite refreshing to behold, said—

"I say, Pipes, old un, you'd better eat 'em while they're hot ; block ornaments ain't good if they once gets cold."

Pipes cast his eyes obliquely towards the plate, and, with a doleful shake of the head, replied—

"I ain't a bit o' happytight, Bob, when my feelin's is onced hurt."

The long youth stretched forth his long right arm, and made a clutch at Pipes' plate.

"Sorry to hear you're so bad, old un," he said, "and it's a pity that good things should be wasted : I'll finish 'em up for you."

Pipes drew the plate away before Long Bob's fingers could close upon the rim.

"I'll try and eat a little bit, Bob," he said ; "not as I thinks I can."

Bob's eyes longingly followed the shreds of meat ; then carefully wiping his plate with the last fragment of his share of the loaf, he remarked—

"It's bad, old un, to eat against your will ; it might give you the indigestion."

Pipes determined to risk the consequences, and in a twinkling his plate was as clean as though it had been unsullied by the contact of the "ornaments."

It was but a sorry meal for those two men and the hungry growing lads ; yet Big Drum, though he possessed the five shillings he had set aside to give the chandler's shop keeper on account, would have gone without food rather than touch one penny piece of the debt.

To Long Bob's suggestion that he should invest a sixpence in beer, Drum answered—

"Mr. Bob—when the man told us he never gave any 'tick, I said to him, ' Out of the very first day's luck you shall have something towards paying what we owes'—and I know it's more than one pun five, so I can't give him less."

"Drum is right," said honest Jack Lennox. "Let us pay off our debts ; then we can eat and drink, and feel all the happier because it will be paid for."

"But only a tanner!" said Bob. "I'll make that up again if we have any luck to-morrow."

Big Drum rose, and taking his hat from the floor, placed it on his head; then, buttoning his coat, marched out of the room, saying—

"Not a coin, Bob. I'll go and pay the men; then you won't have it always before your eyes, which it will be as long as I keeps it here."

Pipes sighed as he beheld Drum walk out with such a mine of wealth in his pocket, and in a sepulchral whisper called out—

"Bob!"

The long youth thrust his hands deep in his empty pockets, and went to his friend's side; and Lily, with her young companion, went to the open window to gaze upward at the small patch of blue sky just discernible amidst the interminable line of hot, dry-looking tiles.

They spoke in low tones of the green lanes around Falconmere Abbey, and, with their arms around each other's necks, spoke hopefully of the mystic future.

"It cannot be always like this," the boy said. "We must bear with it, Lil, until a happier time comes."

"I am happy," she said—and her blue eyes were fixed upon her companion's face—"when I am with you."

"I know you are, Lil; but how can I be so when I see you as you were to-day, limping homeward? I knew your feet were blistered —knew it by the tears that came to your eyes when we had to run across Oxford Street out of the way of an omnibus."

"It did not pain me much, Jack."

"I know better, Lil. You are a brave, good little girl, but you are not fit for the life we have to lead. I wish," he added, "that I were a man, then—then——"

She noted the pause, and, placing her small soft hand upon his shoulder, asked—

"What would you do, Jack?"

He was silent. He had a vague boyish idea that, as a man, he could win both fame and fortune, but how, or by what means, he was at fault.

"I don't know," he said, bluntly; "but I should then be strong and independent, and could work; then, dear Lil, you would live better than you do now."

"I have support," she said, "and Mrs. Smith gives me a very nice bed. What more do I require, Jack?"

"Much," he said; "much more. You have been brought up as a lady; you have had servants to wait upon you; and your slightest wish has been law. After all this, Lil, to have fallen so far beneath your former mode of life, must make you wretched. I know it does me."

"Naughty boy," she said, playfully, "have I not told you I am happy? So why need you make yourself so miserable?"

"You have told me so," he said, moodily, "and I believe you, Lil, but I cannot, when I hear the coarse speaking of these rude men, believe that I am doing right by allowing you to stay with them any longer."

She opened her eyes very wide at this, and was about to speak, but the boy interrupted her by saying—

"I know what you would say, Lil. You feel that these men have been kind to us. They have, I'll admit. Also that, in spite of their manner and appearance, they are honest. But, Lily dear, the life of a street performer, the penury, hardship, and toil, will soon make an inroad upon your delicate health. Then, should you be ill, what will become of us? They will send you to an hospital, and I shall not be able to see you, and—"

His pride gave way under the picture thus conjured up, and leaning his hand upon the window-sill, he burst into tears.

"Jack, dear Jack!"—and she threw her arms around his neck—"do not go on in this manner. We shall be better off soon; I know we shall."

He sobbed out a reply, the words of which were undistinguishable for a time.

"Bob Jawkins," he sobbed, "told me that all this would happen if you were taken to the hospital, and you would have to go, . Lily dear, because we have no money to pay a doctor."

Her soothing words soon won him from his grief, and as he wiped the tears from his eyes, and strove to be cheerful under the bright hopeful words she uttered, a gleam of sunshine lit up the murky chimney-pots.

It was Sol's last ray, as the glorious orb sank with dusky majesty in the far west.

"Look, Jack!" the hopeful child said, "see the sun, how different it makes everything look. Be happy, Jack, under the circumstances in which we are placed, and like the blessed sunshine, happiness of heart will make our path lighter."

"Lily," he said, drawing her to him, "you are a brave girl, and your courageous little heart shames me, who should be of the two the bravest."

"You are brave, dear Jack," she said, caressingly smoothing his forehead, "but your bravery is different to mine."

"How, dear Lil? I don't quite understand you."

"It's this," she said. "When the gipsy came to take us back to the encampment, you fired that dreadful gun at him; that was brave of you—but when you think of the hard life we have you grow miserable, and all your courage leaves you. Not so with me. I could not have shot at that dreadful man, no matter where he had taken me; but though I am often in pain when I dance or walk over these hard hot stones, I wipe away the tears that come to my eyes, and think that some day it will be different, and that thought makes me forget all I have to suffer."

The germ of patient endurance—so strong in the softer sex—was being early developed in this gentle child.

Lily's words gave our hero much thought, and he came to the conclusion that if she could suffer so much uncomplainingly, he could, were he to try, do the same.

He was about to tell her so, when Long Bob's voice startled him.

"Have some!" R. J. shouted, holding a cracked yellow jug above his head. "Come on, young un—do you good."

The dilapidated jug contained nearly a quart of Pipes' favourite mixture—half-and-half.

Jack Lennox took the venerable vessel from R. J., and with careful forethought he poured a little into a handleless teacup for Lily.

"Fancy it's tea," he said to the child, who gently refused it, "it will do you good—do, only a little—there, that's a good girl."

Much to his joy the child moistened her lips with the plebeian beverage, then taking a small portion himself, he gave the jug back to Long Bob.

When Pipes called our long friend to his side, he whispered—

"Like some beer, Bob?"

"Don't aggravate me," answered the youth, " after that beast Drum walking off with five bob in his pocket!"

"That's just it," said Pipes. " Of course he'll go and pay the man the coin, and then they'll have at least one pint over it."

"Hope it'll choke 'em," said Long Bob, charitably; "don't you, Pipes?"

"No, I don't hope that, but I wish I was there to have a share. I say, Bob!"

"Well, old un, say on."

"How does you and the old gal down stairs stand?"

"Pretty well. She wanted me to take her shutter out again."

"Did she?" Pipes said reflectively; "that's a good sign—and lent you the gridiron?"

"Yes."

"Ah! that's another good sign."

"Sign of what? What are you driving at, old un?"

Pipes brought his mouth close to R. J.'s ear and whispered, " Don't you think she'd lend you a bob?"

"Ah!" exclaimed R. J., "good thought! I'll try."

"Do," Pipes said, rubbing his hands; "if she does, bring a pot of the best."

"Like a bird!" said R. J., as he disappeared through the open door.

Whatever arguments he used, they were to the purpose, for, to Pipes' ineffable joy, he came back five minutes afterwards with the beverage.

When Jack Lennox had resigned the precious vessel, Big Drum's footsteps were heard as he ascended the stairs; and Pipes, in his hurry to finish the contents of the jug, nearly suffocated himself.

When Drum entered the room he saw the thin one wiping his eyes with his dirty fingers, and, turning sharply, said, " What, snivelling again, you crocodile, eh?"

"Yes," said Long Bob, readily; "it's tears of joy, Drum. He's thinking of the figure he'll make as Jack-in-the-green."

"Ugh!" growled Drum, "some people can be merry!"

"What's the matter?" asked Bob.

"Not much," Drum replied, heroically; " only the man at the chandler's shop sent for a pint on the strength of the coin I gave him."

"I said so," Pipes whispered.

"And," Drum continued, "I'm blest if the gal didn't fall down and break the jug."

"Of course he sent for another," R. J. said, with a side glance at Pipes; "he couldn't do less."

"Couldn't he?" Drum said, savagely, crushing his hat under his arm. " But he did though, and after me almost fancying I had the taste in my mouth, I didn't get a toothful."

Long Bob and Pipes grinned behind the disappointed one's back.

"Now then, all of you," Drum said, "let's go into the business, 'cos we ain't got much time."

All of them came and gathered round the great man, who thus arranged for the new entertainment.

"Joe Mullins, the sweep," he said, " is coming round to make the green, so it will be all right and up to the mark."

"I say," interrupted Long Bob, " ain't he going to measure Pipes for it?"

"Measure?" Drum said, interrogatively.

"Yes," continued the incorrigible, " I know he'd like it to fit him. My eye, Pipes, won't it be a treat when we beholds your queer-looking mug a grinning through the leaves! Talk about a owl in the ivy bush—ha! ha! ha!"

And R. J. danced a break-down, much to Pipes' annoyance.

"Look here, young fellow," Drum said, " don't you interrupt. I've got all the business in my head, and if you begins your buffoonery it won't be there long, so sit down and be quiet."

Long Bob tried to do so ; but long before Drum had finished the programme, R. J. had slily fastened a pin to the end of a stick, and, much to Pipes' dismay, he received several sharp pricks, and looked beneath the table for the cause.

At last Bob sent the pin with some force into Pipes' leg, and the solo instrumentalist sprang from his chair and gave a yell.

"What's the matter ? " Long Bob calmly asked, as he dropped the stick behind his chair.

"Matter ! " said Pipes, "something stuck in my leg!"

"Order! " shouted Drum. "Now listen, all of you. When we get a good crowd—audience, I mean—you must all keep dancing as long as I plays."

Pipes' face became a woful length as he said—

"But the Jack-in-the-green don't dance with all that lot over him !"

"Don't he ? " said Drum ; "that's where you are wrong. The Green dances longer and quicker than anybody else. So look out, if you don't keep time with me."

"Oh, lor !" gasped Pipes, as he sank into his chair. "I shall never be able to do it !"

Joe Mullins came on the next evening, and tired as the company were, they set to work with a will to help their sooty ally.

The night previous to this new experiment the funds were all exhausted in providing new dresses for the company. Long Bob's get-up was superb, and, as a finish, he drew Pipes' likeness, life-size (the head and face), on the breast of his close-fitting dress.

Drum was in ecstacies with Lily's costume, and declared she looked " stunning ;" as also did Jack in his swallow-tailed coat and lace-bedizened cocked hat.

The only sombre face visible in that little room was Pipes'. He sat as usual, in the darkest corner, casting from time to time savagely spiteful glances towards the green pyramid that seemed to his eyes about as pleasant an object as the rack to a hapless captive in the dungeons of the old Inquisition.

"Beastly thing !" muttered Pipes. "I hope it will all tumble to bits direckly I begins to dance."

His hope was not fulfilled—as, to his sorrow, he discovered before the day was half over.

Never in the course of his existence had his legs moved so nimbly as they did beneath the leafy covering.

Big Drum, having to manage both instruments, had given Long Bob strict orders to keep Pipes a-moving—orders which R. J., in his capacity of clown, found but little difficulty in carrying out.

Poor Pipes, puffing beneath the accumulation of misery which oppressed him, would pause to regain his breath during one of Drum's most spirited passages with the pair of instruments.

In vain, by moving his body to and fro, he sought to keep up a semblance of joining in the dance—the leaves, the artificial flowers moved, but Bob's keen eyes were watching Pipes' square-toed boots, and in an instant he would detect the dodge, and, much to the edification of the bystanders, he would shout, loud enough to be heard above Drum's performance on the instruments—

"Now then, old un, keep it up. Go on—chuck your hoofs about."

The audience would laugh as the green pyramid began to bob about, and then Robert, seizing the opportune moment, would call out—

"Don't forget the coppers, ladies and gentlemen; drop 'em in the ladle. Go round. Lily ; there's a gent has sixpence for you. Keep it up, old un—remember we have got to perform before the Emperor of Roosnia when it comes the first of May in that country."

After thus making the circle into a good humour, he would join hands with Jack and Lily, and the trio, forming a ring, would dance round Pipes until that suffering individual was, as he afterwards declared, ready to drop.

Big Drum's coat pocket began to feel heavy towards night; never in the whole of his "purfessionel" career had he experienced such a day of good luck.

At every pitch they made Lily came to him at its conclusion, with the brass ladle filled with halfpence, and more than once he detected the gleam of a small silver coin among them.

Long Bob, who had danced all day with a vigour that threatened to dislocate his limbs, began to feel weary, and, to Pipes' joy, proposed that they should " cut it."

"One more," Drum said, "opposite that public, then we'll close."

They made a pitch opposite the gin-palace, and when Long Bob gave the signal for the children to join hands, a cry of terror came from Lily's lips, and Jack, raising his eyes, beheld Tinker Tom, his arms crossed upon a post, and his dark sinister eyes glaring vengefully upon the young pair.

The boy gave an angry cry, as he placed himself between Lily and their foe ; then Long Bob, who at once recognized the gipsy by the description Jack had given, clenched his hands, and went towards the burly ruffian.

Tinker Tom would have liked to have seized the boy and girl, but, seeing he was recognized, he turned from them and passed into the public-house.

CHAPTER XIV.
THE DETECTIVE.

WALTER CARLIN traced the fugitives step by step, until he became lost in the mazy windings of the great city.

Then his fondly cherished hopes fell, and, sadder at heart than of yore, he gave up the search.

In one of those quiet streets leading from the Strand to the banks of the polluted Thames, he took apartments.

From his solitary rooms he could wander forth in the hope of yet finding the boy; but day after day passed—each night the weight became heavier upon his heart, and the proud head, before so erect, became drooped, his step less elastic, and among his dark raven locks streaks of glistening grey deepened as the time wore on.

He supped in silence—not a friend had the broken-hearted man to share his misery; and day by day the iron went deeper and deeper to his soul.

During one of his fruitless rambles his eyes caught the inscription upon a brass plate of a door—

"PRIVATE INQUIRY OFFICE."

He repeated the words over and over again, and finally, placing one foot upon the door-step, seemed irresolute whether to enter the dingy office, or pass on to his lonely home.

While thus irresolute, the office door opened, and a grave elderly man was about to pass through.

He came to a sudden standstill when he saw the officer's pale, wan face, and holding the door open, said, blandly—

"Will you step inside?"

Mechanically obeying, Captain Carlin found himself face to face with the clever private detective.

The soldier at once entered upon the matter nearest his heart, and the detective, with a grave smile, drew a chair close to his visitor, and prepared, note-book in hand, to jot down such items as would prove the most useful in the matter.

"I scarcely know," said the officer, "how to begin; in fact, not having contemplated a visit to your office, I am unprepared to state the difficult task I should like you to undertake."

The detective played with his watchguard as he said—

"It requires but little explanation to set my men upon the track of those who have often baffled the most subtle officers from Scotland Yard."

"Indeed!" exclaimed the visitor, startled for a moment by this frank acknowledgment.

"You seem surprised, sir," said the gentlemanly chief of the private detectives, "at my words."

"I am," was the answer.

The chief of the private inquiry office tapped the table with his white fingers.

"You would be more so," he said, "were I to enumerate the series of hidden crimes and the deep mysteries my men have unravelled during the last five years."

"Crimes and mysteries which the regular detectives failed to discover?"

"Even so," was the answer; "now, sir, in what, pray, can I serve you?"

The officer, in as brief terms as possible, related all that is known to the reader, and the grave listener smiled once or twice during the recital.

"I tracked them," said the officer, "from the village near Falconmere until they reached a roadside public house in the southern suburbs of London."

The detective asked the name of the house.

"The Red Lion," answered Captain Carlin; "there I was informed that the children, in company with a youth older than my son, made the acquaintance of two men, who, from the description I have been able to glean, must have been connected with a company of street performers.

Another note was made in the small book, and the detective nodded for his visitor to proceed.

"From that hour," Captain Carlin said, "up to the present time I have failed to discover the least clue."

"I think," the detective said, "I may safely promise that before a week has passed your son will be found and placed in your care."

The officer shook his head sadly, and the detective, noticing the action, said—

"You think I overrate my powers?"

"No," he answered; "but I fear that those upon the boy's track have before this discovered him, and I tremble to think of the consequence."

"Those upon his track—is there more than the vengeful gipsy?"

"There is a Frenchman, who, until the walls of Falconmere fell a prey to the flames, served the earl. Since then he has devoted every energy to the task of finding my boy."

"Have you no idea of his purpose?"

"None."

The detective pondered for a few moments over this statement—then, raising his head, said hopefully—

"Even with this difficulty to cope with, I think I may safely repeat my words."

The soldier's face flushed with joy, and, taking the detective's hand, he exclaimed—

"Do this, and I will reward you beyond your most sanguine expectations."

The detective returned the fervid grasp of his visitor's hand, and said—

"I will do my best."

He rose to open the door for his visitor, and Captain Carlin, turning upon the threshold, asked—

"Can I call daily, and hear how you progress?"

"I think not—no; it will be better not to do so. Should anything occur that leads me to the belief that we may conclude our task before the week has expired, I will send to you."

"Be it so; I will hopefully await the passing of the next six days."

He turned from the door-step, his pale, careworn face looking brighter than it had for many weeks.

The detective watched his visitor until he passed from view; then, re-entering the office, he looked carefully over the notes he had made.

"There will be no difficulty," he thought, "if we can get possession of the gipsy—the Frenchman, too; he must have some motive in thus closely following the children. What can it be?"

A few moments' thought suggested a trap to catch Monsieur Jules Latour.

Rapidly the pen glided over the paper as he wrote—

"If the French gentleman who followed two children from Bridgenorth to London will call at the Private Inquiry Office, No. 1, ——, he will hear something to his advantage."

Pressing the white knob of a call-bell, a lad appeared from an inner room.

"Take this," the chief said; "write it out, and leave a copy with each of the daily papers."

The lad took the paper, bowed, and disappeared behind the noiseless baize-covered door.

"So much for the Frenchman," he thought; "now for the gipsy."

He pondered long over many plans to lure Tinker Tom to the private inquiry office, but knowing the ways of these wanderers, he dismissed plan after plan as hopeless.

"The same bait," he thought, "that may hook the Frenchman will not get a nibble from the gipsy."

Striking the call-bell twice brought a stout, well-dressed man to his presence.

"I'm glad you are not out, Harvey," the chief said, "for I have a case that is peculiarly in your line."

He explained a portion of the captain's statement to his subordinate, and when describing the strolling players, a smile passed over the man's features.

"I do not think," the chief said, "that it will be necessary to go out of London to find these men."

"I think not."

"Should you find them, bring the boy away at once—that is," he added, "if they are together. If not, go at once upon his track, and do not return here without him."

The man bowed, and left the office. As he passed through the busy street he muttered—

"Big Drum and Pipes, for a thousand pounds! I wonder what they will think of their old friend in his new line. Poor old boys! I'll warrant Pipes has shed many tears since we parted."

The well-dressed agent was the ungrateful Buffler.

Passing the Mansion House, a boy of the Shoeblack Brigade touched his hat to the private detective.

"Clean your boots, sir?" then, in an under tone, "have 'em cleaned; I've seen him."

The Buffler nodded, and the boy, taking his box a few paces down a quiet turning, spread his brushes out, and turning up the bottoms of his customer's trousers—a very long job, by the way, in this instance—

"I watched for him," the boy said, while the Buffler, with an affected carelessness, watched the vehicles as they whirled past, "but he didn't come till this morning."

"Ha! what hour?"

"About ten, sir."

"Proceed."

The right boot was being elaborately blackened by this time.

"He came up the steps from Thames Street," said the boy, "and at the side of the bridge which is just over where the steamer goes from, he met a man."

"Describe him."

"A stout-built fellow. I could not see much of his face, because he had a seal-skin cap pulled over his forehead."

"Well?"

"I tried, though, and as I asked them to have their boots cleaned, I saw that the man with the cap had a mark across his cheek."

"A red streak?"

"Yes, sir."

"Timothy Adkins," muttered the Buffler. "I thought there was more than one in the job. Well, boy, what became of them?"

"The man with the mark on his cheek and the fair nice-looking young gentleman walked to the railway station."

The private detective bit his lip.

"I followed them, and luckily a gent had

his boots cleaned close under the place where they give out the tickets."

"Yes, yes."

"I heard the man with the cap say, 'Boulogne,' and the young gentleman gave him a brown pocket-book. That's all, sir."

"What became of the youngest ?"

"He called a hansom, and went away, just as the train started."

The boots were by this time finished, and the boy's eyes sparkled as two half-crown pieces were placed in his hand.

"You have done well," said the agent, "I have another job for you."

"Yes, sir;" and as he slipped the coins in his pocket the begrimed but intelligent face became very pleased in its expression.

"Have you seen any street performers lately ?" the agent asked.

The boy reflected for a few moments before he answered—

"Yes, sir; several."

"Describe them."

"Yesterday there was a man with a monkey and a——"

"No use. The party I want,' I have every reason to believe, will consist of four—two men, a boy, and a girl."

"Tumblers, sir ?"

"The boy most likely will do that; the girl, I expect, will dance, and the two men —one short and stout, and the other tall and thin—the stout one will have a drum, the other a mouth-organ, and, in all likelihood, a small box suspended round his neck by a strap."

The boy shook his head, and said—

"I ain't seen 'em, sir. The last lot I saw was up Shoreditch way; but that was Jack-in-the-green day."

"It was not those I seek."

"No, sir; but there was a fat man with a drum, two boys, and such a pretty little girl, besides a man doing Jack-in-the-green."

The private detective reflected for some minutes.

"In numbers," he thought, "they seem to tally with the chief's description. But I should scarcely expect Drum would leave his legitimate line for this."

"The little girl," the shoeblack said, breaking in upon the detective's thoughts, "had the most beautifullest hair in the world —all like gold, and hung down her back a long way ?"

"Her description!" exclaimed the detective, struck by the boy's words. "Well, the boys—what were they like ?"

"One was bigger than the other, and an awful cheeky one, too. He kept chaffing the people and the man inside the green, but the other boy did not say a word; I don't think he looked as though he liked the job."

"Perhaps not. Well—about the man with the drum."

"He was short and fat, and wore a white dirty hat with a black band round it."

"How did he wear it ?"

The boy looked up, rather puzzled at this interrogation.

"I mean," the detective said, "did he wear it drawn over his eyes, on the back of his head, or how !"

"Neither," the boy answered; "now I remember, it was all on one side."

"Big Drum !" muttered the agent; "this boy is invaluable."

"Is it them, sir ?" asked the shoeblack, the prospect of two similar coins to those he already possessed looming pleasantly in the distance.

"I hope so," was the reply. "Now, Sam, you must leave off cleaning boots to-day, and try what you can find out about the Jack-in-the-green party."

"Yes, sir; what am I do ?"

"You saw them, you say, near Shoreditch ?"

"Yes, sir."

"Well, you go among the keepers of the stalls which line the road, and inquire. Some one is sure to have seen them—follow every clue you may get, and if possible discover where they live."

"Yes, sir—where shall I see you ?"

"I will be opposite the railway station in Bishopsgate at nine o'clock."

"Very well, sir; I will be there. If I meet them to-day, what shall I do ?"

"Do not lose sight of them until they are safely housed."

"All right, sir !"

Then, throwing his box on his back, the boy dived among the crowd of vehicles and disappeared.

The private detective walked quickly to the telegraph office at the railway station and much surprised the clerk by sending the following message to a brother officer at Dover :—

"Adkins—en route for Boulogne—brown leather pocket-book—scar over cheek—sealskin cap—packet leaves 10 this evening— the other safe yet—parted this morning."

He paid for the transmission of the message, and left the clerk wondering what sort of people they were who could make anything out of the above message.

The detective paused outside the telegraph office, undecided which way to turn.

He had great confidence in his young ally, and believed that the boy would do as much good as far as the search was concerned as he could.

"He can work the west-end to-day," thought the agent; "I'll take a turn southward."

Passing over the bridge, his mind reverted to the different cases which had so completely baffled the regular and the private detectives.

A merchant's office safe had been broken open, and the contents stolen; but, strange to say, the office door and the outer doors bore no marks of having been forced; yet the robber or robbers must have passed through them before reaching the safe.

The peculiar construction of the locks put an end to the blue-coated officials' hypothesis that the thieves had entered by using skeleton keys.

When the case was given over to the head of the private detectives, the Buffler joined Big Drum and Pipes, in order that he could watch the movements of the merchant's son.

For upon this youth the detective's suspicion fell.

He alone had charge of the keys, and they were morally certain that the young fellow had a share in the robbery.

But how to prove it?

The merchant's son was under his father's roof from the time the office was closed until the next morning, and the keys were in his possession—so he stated—the whole time.

It was a case that required the most delicate handling, and the Buffler, as he called himself when he joined Drum's company, took charge of the affair.

He spent a month with the street performers, but without gleaning the least clue to the mystery.

Other matters compelled him to suddenly leave his friends, and the chief, looking upon the affair as undiscoverable, gave the Buffler another case.

The latter's pride was a little touched by his failure, and though he entered upon the new affair, he had not lost sight of the old one.

The detectives, to glean information, are compelled to use peculiar means.

Costermongers, crossing-sweepers, and shoeblacks are very useful to them.

The Buffler took one of the latter, and pointed out the merchant's son to him, and told the boy to watch him closely.

The result has been detailed.

Adkins, a returned convict, had been seen lurking near the office by the detective, when performing at the corner of the street.

To find out the suspicious-looking fellow's name was easily accomplished by the Buffler.

To link this man's appearance with the robbery was easy, and the detective's mind at once grasped the whole facts of the case.

But ere he could act upon his conviction it was necessary to obtain a proof of the collusion between the merchant's son and Timothy Adkins.

The shoeblack had obtained this, and as the agent walked slowly towards the Borough, his eyes searching for his old companions, his thoughts were occupied with the bullion robbery.

"It's as clear as the noonday's sun," he mentally argued; "the lad is rather fast—fond of billiard-rooms and betting; the old fellow has a due regard for the value of £ s. d.—the boy wants money—he lends Adkins the keys of the outer doors—the safe is broken open, and none's the wiser for his share in the affair—so he imagines; but the clumsiness of the key business betrayed him. Now, how am I to act? Will the father hush up the affair for his son's sake, or—— ?"

"Rub-a-dub-dub, toot-te-to-toot."

From the depths of a narrow turning came the sounds of a drum and a mouth-organ, and the detective, postponing the solution of the question he had begun to argue, started in the direction of the sound.

CHAPTER XV.

THE BOUNDING BROTHERS OF BARCELONA.

THE appearance of Tinker Tom put our "purfessionel" friends on their guard, and as they dragged their tired limbs through the bye-streets en route to Mrs. Smith's hospitable mansion, Lily was closely guarded by her companions.

One small hand was drawn through Jack's arm, and tightly clasped by the bold, handsome boy.

Long Bob walked in front, the heavy brass ladle gripped ready for instant use should the foe make his appearance. R. J., though somewhat loosely put together, was possessed of wondrous muscular power, and armed as he was, Tinker Tom would have found his master had he attempted to take the girl from their keeping.

Big Drum and his tired friend brought up the rear—Drum elated at the weight of his pockets—Pipes depressed in consequence of having to carry home the leafy covering he had suffered under for so many hours.

Except having to endure the cutting remarks of various boys, our friends reached home without any event worthy of recording.

A rest and some refreshment did them much good; then Drum, in the capacity of orchestra, manager, secretary, general director, and treasurer, began to count over the day's receipts.

The number of threepenny, fourpenny, and sixpenny pieces he found among the copper coins, for some time took away his breath and stayed the counting.

"I'm blest," he remarked, looking fondly at the little heaps, "if this ain't a good day's work!"

"How much is there?" Long Bob asked.

"In silver?" questioned Drum.

"No, altogether," said R. J., mildly.

"There ain't any bad uns—the silver 'mounts to nineteen and tenpence."

Pipes pricked up his ears and began to entertain visions of numberless pots of the "favourite."

"The coppers," Drum continued, "'mounts to eleven and sevenpence ha'penny—that's, how much altogether, Jack?"

"One pound eleven shillings and fivepence halfpenny," the boy answered, readily.

Pipes wiped his mouth with the dirty fringe, and Long Bob stood upon his head in the centre of the room, and the children, who looked upon this amount as a fortune, clapped their hands joyfully.

"One pun' eleven and fippence ha'penny," said Drum; "the one pun' must go to the shop round the corner—the rest we divides."

Pipes pulled a long face at this, and R. J. came to his feet much quicker than he had intended.

"I think," Drum continued, "it will be the best way for us to have two bob a-piece, and put the extra one five and a half away."

"Look here, Drum," said Long Bob, "can't you give the cove ten bob less and pay the rest afterwards?"

Big Drum shook his head.

"No, Bob," he replied; "it won't allers be the fust of May—I wish it was."

"Does you?" said Pipes; "I don't, then."

"Hold your noise, shadder; we's talking about business."

The shadder subsided, and Drum resumed—

"It's this way, you see, Bob; arter that black-looking gipsy chap being so close upon us to-day, I don't think it will be safe to stay in the streets—not as we need care much, but it's our little gal we must look arter."

"Right, Drum," Long Bob said; "we must look after her, but what are we to do?"

"This is what I've been thinking," Drum continued; "there will be a fair going on at a little town I know not far out of London—s'pose we works our way down there—and if we is lucky we can get enough to start a booth, eh—what do you think of that?"

"Capital," said R. J. "But we must get up some sort of performance to draw the yokels."

"That's just it, Bob; now what can we do?"

Long Bob's inventive genius soon solved the matter.

"Look here, Drum," he said, "of course we shall have to make a show outside."

"Exactly."

"And to get the people around we must have a big picture on the outside of our booth."

"Yes, Bob, that must be done—but what can we put on it?"

"There's plenty of things we might have; for example—Pipes might be the Living Skeleton, and we could get a penny extra by admitting the public to see him drink beer."

Pipes shuffled about on his seat; he did not particularly relish being shown as a living skeleton, but the beer-drinking part of the programme made him hope the arrangement would be carried into effect.

"No," Drum said, "the public don't care much for these sort of things—they have had plenty of skeletons and fat women lately. Can't you think of something else?"

"Yes," R. J. said, giving Pipes a mischievous glance, "we can blacklead the old un all over, and stick up, 'To be seen alive, the great and mighty chief of Jumbo Island;' and when the people come in and begin to wonder how it is he is so thin, you can tell 'em that it is in consequence of the chief not having any of his wives to roast and eat for breakfast that makes him so."

The idea was not a bad one, Drum thought, yet it was not the thing.

"Look here, Bob," he said, "what's you and the young uns to do?"

"Oh, we'll do the outside. I'll be clown, Jack can be harlequin, and Lily columbine."

"Yes," Drum said; "but ain't there anything else?"

"I hopes there is," whispered Pipes, "'cos I ain't going to be blackleaded when there ain't no beer in the part I has to perform."

Long Bob drew his considering cap well over his head, and after a few minutes' pause he slapped Drum on the back and called out—

"Yes; I've got it!"

"Where, Bob, where?"

"Here, down in my nut, and I think it will do to rights."

Drum hoped it would, and prepared himself to receive the long youth's brilliant thought.

"This is it," said Bob: "we'll have stuck up in large letters, 'This way to the Bounding Brothers of Barcelona and the Young Princess of the Thigamybob Mountains.'"

"That'll look fine," said the delighted manager; "and if we gets a trumpet, Pipes can shout it out every minute while I goes on with the music."

"Yes," said Bob enthusiastically; "we must have three dresses, you know, Drum: one to do the outside business, and the others to do the Bounding Brothers of Barcelona."

Drum saw the necessity for this, and at

LONG BOB AND PIPES TO THE RESCUE.

once began to plan how the material for the dresses was to be obtained.

Long Bob's skill was of great use to the company in making up the material, and, to do him justice, he did the work wonderfully well, considering how little he had learnt from the gin-drinking little tailor.

He tried hard to have poor Pipes black-leaded and transformed into the terrible chief of Jumbo Island, but Drum over-ruled this, much to the slender one's relief.

"We can't very well do it, Bob," said Drum, "in conserkance of wanting the shadder outside to holler through the trumpet."

"I don't see why we couldn't. He could just as well wash his face, and come out, as not."

"No, Bob; it ain't to be thought on. Why, he'd have to wash hisself every time, and the washing would be too much for him."

"Why?"

"Because," said Big Drum, with a grin, "by the time he had got hisself washed like that, he would only be the size of this here drumstick handle."

"I say," whispered Pipes, "when you is both done making game of me, p'raps you'll leave off."

"All right, old un," said R. J.; "you don't know what good things we shall have for you."

"Had quite enough of good things for one day," said Pipes, spitefully. "So if you thinks to blacklead me all over, you won't."

"Shut up!" said Drum; "we don't want your spoke in the business. I think the best thing you can do is to go out and sell the green."

"What! that——"

"Yes. Somebody will buy it, if it's only for the timber that's in it."

"Whether anybody 'ud buy it or not," Pipes said, "I won't take it out."

Big Drum's fury was ungovernable. To be thus set at defiance by his hitherto meek companion caused his very nose to turn blue; so, before Pipes could finish his defiant answer, Drum's white hat struck him across the mouth.

Long Bob wanted to back the old un to go in for a little of the fistic business, but Pipes would not come up to the scratch.

* * * * *

The appearance of Big Drum's company at the fair excited the envy of less fortunate proprietors than our stout red-nosed friend.

From morn to closing time the front of the booth was crowded by a closely-packed collection of grinning rustics.

Long Bob became brilliant as clown, and sorely chaffed the chawbacons who did not comply with his request to "walk up."

Jack Lennox made a splendid harlequin, and little Lily, as columbine, caused many exclamations of admiration from the crowd.

Big Drum was in the seventh heaven, as, seated behind his drum, he belaboured the parchment.

Pipes had wrapped his mouth-organ carefully in brown paper, and appeared behind a huge speaking-trumpet; and when Drum gave him an opportunity, he refreshed the crowd by making the most unearthly noises.

It might have been an imitation of a man with a sore throat, or a dying bull's roar; yet it was not either; and though many a puzzled agricultural gentleman asked another agricultural ditto, "What this chap be doing with the horn?" they could not obtain a decided answer.

A piece of canvas, stretched, as Long Bob observed, from "pole to pole," bore this telling announcement in large black letters—

"*The Great Rung, and the Bounding Brothers of Barcelona! The Young Princess, from the Thingamy Mountains. Walk up! One Penny each to see the whole of the performance!!*"

Nearly opposite Big Drum's show, a powerful rival had taken his stand, and the following announcement drew many eyes from the feats of the "Bounding Brothers of Barcelona"—

"*The Laughing Pig! also the Calculating Pug! Alive! Alive!*"

The first hour or so after the company had thrown open their show, Long Bob saw with dismay that the Laughing Pig and his friend the Calculating Pug drew tremendously, and in spite of Drum's performance, Pipes' trumpets, and his own splendid wit, the crowd, after gaping with open mouths at the exterior of the show would ungratefully walk to the rival exhibition.

"This'll never do, Drum," said Bob; "that feller takes all the custom."

Drum looked wistfully at a small crowd who were cheerfully paying their pennies to behold the Pig and the Pug.

"It won't, Bob," he said; "is there any paint left?"

"The black paint Pipes used for the canvas?"

"Yes, Bob."

"There is a little, Drum. How much do you want?"

"Not much; only enough to stick up a fresh attraction that'll smash that feller."

"Him with the Pug?"

"Yes. Fetch the paint, Bob, and we'll get Pipes to write up—'The Talking Herring—the Dancing Helephant—and the Whistling Crab.'"

"That won't do," suggested Pipes, "unless we have something to show like 'em."

"You'll do for the Herring," said Drum, savagely.

"And you," Pipes retorted, "will make a fine Helephant."

Long Bob, Jack, and Lily were highly amused at this, and Jack suggested—

"Bob, as Drum and Pipes will manage their parts, suppose I personate the Crab?"

"Can't see how it is to be done, young un. You might do the Crab by going outside and whistling through the canvas, but the Elephant and the Herring is too much."

"No, it ain't," growled Drum. "We can, after you three have gone through your performance, set up a cry, and say the Helephant has broke loose."

"Good," said Bob, "that will do. Now, old un, fetch the paint, and go at it; we'll spiflicate the Pug in no time!"

Beneath the first announcement, Pipes added—

"*Also the Laughing Herring—the Dancing Elephant—and the Whistling Crab. One Penny admittance to the whole entertainment.*"

"Talking Herring," said Drum, pointing to the alteration; "you've put laughing."

"That will do much better," Long Bob said. "Now, then, here come some chawbacons; go it, music; now, Jack and Lil, let's have a round."

They joined hands and spun round, to the sepulchral groanings of Pipes' trumpet and the deafening noise of the drum.

The fresh announcement and this display soon drew a crowd; then Long Bob came forward, and pointing to a rustic youth whose sturdy frame was arrayed in a dirty yellow smock-frock, said—

"Come back again, have you?"

The rustic opened his mouth very wide—he had not been near the show until now.

"What a mouth!" Long Bob said. "I shouldn't like to be a potato——"

"I say," one of the bystanders called out, "where do you keep the elephant?"

Long Bob was quite ready for this query.

"Well," he asked, "where do you think?"

"Dunno—don't believe you've got one."

"Come," R. J. answered, "I'll bet you a sovereign we have—here, will any gentleman hold the money?"

No gentleman came forward, and Bob, to convince the sceptics respecting their possession of the huge animal, whispered as he passed Pipes—

"Put your trumpet inside, old un; I must go and make the elephant roar."

During the time the crowd were laughing at Long Bob's sallies, Pipes slipped inside and took his instrument out of brown paper, and left the speaking-trumpet inside the doorway.

"All right," he whispered behind Long Bob, "just in the doorway."

This announcement Bob turned to advantage by answering Pipes and talking at the crowd.

"Broken loose, did you say, and dancing all over the place? I'll soon settle him."

R. J. made a frantic rush inside the show, and, placing the trumpet to his mouth with one hand, with the other he seized a hammer and began beating the seats as an accompaniment to the bellowings of the trumpet.

The crowd were convinced of the elephant's existence, and many began to speculate upon the outlay to view the whole of the entertainment.

Long Bob wound up the business in a most effectual manner by swinging the elephant's trunk two or three times across the open doorway.

"There he be! there he be!" exclaimed one, as Bob gave a louder roar through the trumpet, and again his long trunk was seen.

"He be fightin' wi' 'im," remarked another. Our long friend, ever ready-witted, had stuffed one of the sleeves of his jacket with shavings, and, trusting to the deep shadow, he swayed it about inside.

Truth to tell, Big Drum and the remainder of the company were much more astonished by this sight than were the crowd.

Big Drum so much so, that he rapped his fingers on the edge of the drum; Pipes stood watching the dusky-looking affair, evidently wondering what it was, how it came there, and feeling thankful that Long Bob had joined their company.

"I've quieted him," said R. J. as he came to the front. "Now, gentleman, walk up, walk up—it's getting near dinner time—if you don't come now you will be sorry—this way, sir, pass inside, sir—we'll collect the money inside—go it music—now Jack, another round—hold tight, Lil—the elephant's trunk did the business. Eh! what was it? The sleeve of my old jacket!"

"Bravo!" Jack said, softly, "there they go, we must have at least twenty inside."

"The crib will hold sixty—loose hands and do a jig."

Pipes wheezed and squeaked upon the mouth organ—Drum belaboured the parchment—and the trio danced until they were breathless.

A loud bang on the drum brought the outside performance to a close, and during the time occupied by Pipes in collecting the money, Long Bob and our hero were beneath the stage, changing their dress preparatory to appearing as the Bounding Brothers of Barcelona.

The audience were too thick-skulled to applaud or condemn the performance; so with mouths agape, they sat until the Bounding Brothers had concluded, and little Lily, her graceful form draped with rose-coloured gauze, was led forward by Jack Lennox.

The hobnailed gentry were not proof against the child's winning grace and faultless face and form.

They did not clap their hands, shuffle their feet, whistle, or yell "Encore!" when the girl retired, but in lieu of those demonstrations so peculiarly the fashion of the town gods, Messrs. Baconrind, Fatpork, and Co., looked after the child, and remarked—

"She be a pretty un—don't 'ee think so, Giles?"

"Ees, lad, she look purty loike, but these darned play actor people do look loike that when they be dressed up."

"Hold thee tongue, lad; there be t'elephunt coming."

"Whur?"

"Don't 'ee hear un roaring loike mad?"

"Ees, I do. Here comes young chap to tell us summat."

Jack Lennox came to the front of the rough stage, and making a profound bow, said boldly—

"Gentleman, I am requested by the manager to tell you the elephant is, from some unknown cause, very savage just now; and when in that state it is dangerous to bring him out of his cage."

Long Bob, who was behind the canvas back of the stage, gave a succession of unearthly moans through the trumpet.

"That noise, gentlemen," little Jack resumed, "is the elephant's cry when he is angry."

"Bring un out," shouted a red-headed farmer's lad; "we paid our money to see un, and it don't matter to us if he be savage."

"We should have much pleasure in doing so," said Jack, coolly, "but we dare not endanger the lives of the people by——"

Here Long Bob gave a most terrible roar.

"You hear that," Jack continued, scarcely able to refrain from laughing outright. "He's getting worse every minute."

"Where's t' herring, then?" asked the rustic Rufus; "*that* bean't savage too?"

"No," Jack said, "but unfortunately the elephant is now standing over the glass dish which contains the herring, and we dare not take it away."

"Where's t' crab, then?"

"The crab?" Jack said—"Hush!"

The rustics held their breath and listened, as Long Bob began to whistle through a hole in the canvas.

"Bring un out—bring un out!" shouted the discontented portion of the audience.

Now was the moment for Long Bob to interpose and save the credit of the company.

Rushing upon the stage, armed with a hammer, he began striking wildly at about an inch of the stuffed sleeve which Pipes kept lolling through a rent in the canvas.

"There be his trunk, lookee!" exclaimed one; "he'll be coming out directly."

"Run about, Jack," whispered Bob, "then make a bolt towards the chawbacons."

Jack got up a good counterfeit of sudden terror, and after running to and fro the narrow limits of the stage, asked, loud enough for the audience to hear—

"Is he loose?"

Big Drum, who had the trumpet, made a terrific noise through it; Pipes moved the stuffed sleeve quickly about behind the canvas; Lily gave a scream, and Long Bob, as he plied his hammer, shouted—

"Yes, he's broken his chain—run, Jack, and fasten the doors; if he gets out he will kill every stranger he——"

This, coupled with Jack's sudden flight towards the door, had the desired effect. In an instant every rustic sprang to his feet, and, amid cries and shouts of fear, they rushed madly towards the door.

Big Drum kept them to it by sending forth such fearful growls through the speaking trumpet as caused the panic to increase, and the show was emptied in a wonderfully short space of time.

The last of the gulled yokels had disappeared before the sensation was brought to a conclusion.

Then the company, no longer able to contain their long-suppressed feeelings, gave way to shout after shout of laughter.

"That may do for once," Long Bob remarked; "but we must not come it again."

"What's to be done?" asked Drum. "You see it didn't draw without having something else besides the Bounding Brothers and the Fairy Princess."

"That's true," said Bob; "it shows their bad taste. I don't see anything that we can do, unless we get up another dodge."

Drum rubbed the tip of his nose reflectively.

"Look here!" Long Bob continued, "I have it!"

"Eh! have you?"

"Yes, Drum. We'll get up a terrific combat between the Wild Elephant of Nova Scotia and the Daring Hunter of the Chumchum Forest!"

"That sounds well," remarked Pipes. "Now, how is it to be done?"

"Very easy, old 'un. I'll go over to the man that let us have this booth, and borrow an old cowhide I saw there."

"Good," Drum assented. "You'll dress yourself up, eh?"

"Yes, and Pipes can work away with the

stuffed sleeve; and if I can get an old hatchet we shall do."

"We shall, Bob."

The fame of the whistling crab and the enraged elephant having spread after the first performance, the company found it impossible, in consequence of a sudden rush of visitors, to put the Daring Hunter of the Chum-chum Forest upon the stage.

Agricultural gentlemen began to pour in—some in cow-gowns; others in waistcoats and ties of all colours that were known and unknown some (and these were accompanied by ruddy-cheeked Venuses) came in white hats, the nap a good inch in length, and standing out defiantly.

The second audience demanded the production of the laughing herring and the whistling crab—they were satisfied respecting the elephant; they ought to have been, for the animal's roar was tremendous, and the manner in which he beat his trunk against the canvas caused many a scream from the female patrons.

Bob took advantage of these sounds of fear, and Jack was deputed to go forward and make a speech.

"Ladies and gentlemen," he said, "we are sorry that we cannot bring forward the laughing fish and his companion the whistling crab, in consequence of the elephant, whose roar you can hear, and whose trunk you may observe beating against the canvas, as he madly tries to get hold of his keeper and crunch him up. This savage beast, ladies and gentlemen, will not allow us to touch his companions, but if you will be silent, you shall hear them go through their performance."

There was a little outburst of dissatisfaction, but it was soon quelled by the rustic Venuses taking Jack's part.

When everything was quiet, they heard the herring laugh (Pipes), and the crab whistle a tune (Long Bob); and much to the satisfaction of the company the audience retired, fully satisfied with the entertainment set before them.

CHAPTER XVI.

LILY IN TINKER TOM'S POWER.

A REPETITION of these dodges brought the first day's performance to a satisfactory close, and with bright hopes of the morrow the company partook of a sumptuous supper before retiring.

Drum and his thin friend slept upon a pile of straw in one corner of the stage: Long Bob and Jack, upon a similar shake-down, stretched their weary limbs in the opposite corner.

The little girl had quite a tasteful retreat at the back of the stage. Jack Lennox and Bob had devoted many hours to the construc-

tion and fittings of the fairy princess's chamber.

True, it was but a tiny space, and the sides were but canvas; but the boys had cunningly concealed the dingy reality by sundry strips of pink glazed calico.

They had also erected a bedstead with a few pieces of wood, and this, with a little flock bed and a blanket, made, under the circumstances, a very comfortable apartment.

Poor child!—had it been the hard, cold ground, she would have slept quite as soundly. The dancing outside had completely exhausted her tender frame, and scarcely had her wearied head touched the pillow when her eyes closed, and she fell into a deep sleep.

Everything remained quiet until near daybreak; then the tired company were suddenly aroused by the fearful alarm of fire.

They were upon their feet in a second, and simultaneously a cry of horror came from their lips as they beheld the canvas at the back of the stage burst into a sudden blaze.

"Lily!" exclaimed Jack, as he dashed towards the place, "Lily, wake up, or you will be burnt."

No answer—no response to his wild appeal; and the boy, trembling with a dread apprehension that his little companion had fallen a victim to the suffocating smoke which hid her resting-place from his view, rushed madly forward and tore down the canvas.

The bed was empty, and part of her clothes, neatly folded, lay upon a small box beside it.

The lad was dazed, bewildered, and held spell-bound at this mystic disappearance; and had not Long Bob suddenly pulled him away, he would have been scorched by the rapidly rising flames.

"Lily," exclaimed Long Bob, "is she——"

He could not utter the dreadful word—it seemed too horrible—to ask if that fairy young creature had died!

Jack Lennox's manner suggested the worst; his head had drooped upon his breast, and his hands were compressed tightly across his eyes, as though to shut out some dreadful sight.

In a voice choked and husky he said—

"She is gone—gone, taken away!"

Long Bob breathed freely.

"It might have been worse," he said. "Cheer up, Jack, we shall soon find her again. Come, Drum, give me a hand, and let's pull down this part of the booth before the fire catches it."

A few minutes sufficed to stay the progress of the flames, and, save for the back of the stage being destroyed, there was little damage done.

An event like this soon caused the proprietors and others connected with the various booths and shows to assemble, and with that kindness which the poor at all times show to the poor, a proposal was at once set forward and acted upon.

It was for all to set to work and repair the damage, each booth proprietor to contribute a certain amount of wood and canvas.

Many hands make light work ; and so before the day had fully dawned the still smouldering canvas was replaced, and but for the sudden loss they had sustained, the company would have returned to that state from which they were so rudely aroused.

Unconscious of all that passed, Jack Lennox sat upon one of the seats, his heart heavy and his eyes wet with tears.

A bluff, red-faced man, the proprietor of a caravan wherein was to be seen a giant eight feet two inches high (the caravan was not six from floor to ceiling), placed his hand upon Jack's shoulder and roughly but kindly asked the cause of his grief.

The boy looked up, but he could not speak ; so Long Bob, who stood near our hero, answered for him—

"A little girl," he said, "that we had with us, has disappeared very strangely—it preys on his mind, sir."

"The child that danced outside ? "

"Yes, sir."

The red-faced man brought his open hand smartly down upon his leg, and made use of a very strong expletive.

"I thought," he said, "I knew the child again ; I saw her, when the crib was on fire, in the company of a man."

"A man !" Long Bob repeated ; "a man ? Was she going willingly ? "

"I did not notice, but I saw them coming from the fire as I ran out."

"Tinker Tom has got her," said Pipes huskily ; "poor little girl !"

"Did you," Long Bob asked, "notice the man at all, sir ? "

"No ; he passed me so quickly, and had the little girl by the hand. But now I come to think of it, he had gaiters on, and seemed to limp as he walked."

Long Bob looked from Big Drum to Pipes as he muttered—

"He's got her at last !"

There could be no doubt now poor Lily was in the hands of her most inveterate foe, and the trio—for poor Jack took no part in the conversation—talked in a low tone about the poor child's danger.

Big Drum would have set forth at once in pursuit of the abductor, but Pipes and Bob dissuaded him from it.

"It won't do any good," Bob said. "We shall do better by being quiet for a day or so."

"I don't see that," said Drum.

"It's this way," Bob said ; "if we follow him at once he will take good care to keep

out of the way, but if we remain quiet he may come here again and try to get Jack. If he does we shall be able to get her back."

"Very well," Drum said ; "I gives in, but I don't think we shall ever see her again."

"Never !" sobbed Jack. "Poor Lily !"

The council ended with a resolution to give that day to the fair, and to start early next morning in quest of the loved and lost Lily.

Poor Jack suffered the most acute anguish when performing, and the day seemed as though it never would end.

Long Bob, although his heart was sad, seemed ten times more witty than ever as he stood upon the platform bandying words with the crowd.

Roars of laughter followed his description of the bellowing of the elephant, together with his companions, the whistling crab and the laughing fish.

This part of the entertainment they were compelled to give up ; none had the heart to carry on the humorous deception of the previous day.

The show drew wonderfully. The report of the fire had made the place popular, and crowds came to view the interior—to behold the ravages the fire had made, as much as to see the performance.

There was a choking feeling in Long Bob's throat as he facetiously told the next crammer—that the elephant had with a wondrous sagacity taken the laughing herring and the whistling crab upon his back, and escaped with them during the fire.

Towards evening they found the audience becoming smaller and beautifully less each representation.

Little wonder, for the Bounding Brothers of to-day, and the light, elastic forms of the previous day, were totally different.

"Look here, Drum," Long Bob said, at last, and the tears came to his eyes as he spoke ; "we can't stand any more of this, so let's pack up, and go in search of poor Lil."

Jack Lennox pressed his hand in silent thankfulness, for though the chance was but small of recovering the sweet child, yet the fact of being in search of her would be better than remaining there another day.

So the booth was taken down and returned to the owner ; then, with heavy hearts and bowed heads, they left the noisy scene to go in quest of the sunny child whose gentle manners had won the strong love of these rough men, and made her loss so deeply felt that they would have faced any danger to free her from her captivity.

Long Bob said but little ; but there was an expression in his eyes that boded ill for Tinker Tom, should they meet.

So they commenced their search; every child's form they saw in the distance causing a throb of pain and disappointment when they found it was not the loved and lost Lily.

CHAPTER XVII.

THE CAPTIVE.

TINKER TOM, like a sleuth-hound, had dogged the steps of the company since the day he had beheld Lily and Jack performing in the street transformation scene.

The vow the gipsy had so solemnly registered was not forgotten, and, sleeping or waking, he looked forward with savage joy to the moment which should place the helpless girl in his power.

Gloatingly he crouched behind the canvas booth, and when night came upon the earth he cut an opening through the frail covering and crept inside.

With the panther's wary gait, and a fierce dusky gleam in his eyes, he stole to the little slumberer's bedside, and gazed with fiendish triumph upon his victim.

"Safe," he muttered, as he opened a clasp-knife. "When I have settled the young serpent who stung me, I will come for you."

Prowling noiselessly about the stage, he came to Jack Lennox's wretched couch, and so great was the joy that filled his heart he could scarce repress a cry of exultation.

The pale moonlight, shining through an opening in the roof, fell upon the boy's handsome face, and that of his companion, the quaint but good-hearted Bob Jawkins.

There was murder in the gipsy's heart as he stooped over the prostrate form, and but for Bob being suddenly disturbed in his sleep, the gleaming knife would have done its fell work.

Long Bob started as the gipsy placed his hand upon the bed-covering, and, half rising, muttered—

"Stir up the elephant, Jack; stir him up!"

The words were scarcely distinguishable, and the intended assassin, his evil thoughts rendering him a coward, thought he was awake and speaking to his companion, and glided away as noiselessly as he came.

Standing motionless for some time, he waited, ready to spring upon the first that came towards him, until Bob's mutterings ceased. Then, afraid to return and complete the deed his diabolical passion had prompted him to contemplate, he crept to the back of the stage and struck a silent congreve.

Applying this to a small coil of well-tarred hemp, he set fire to the canvas, and, as the flames began to spread, he again went to Lily's bedside.

He made a small bundle of the child's clothing, then, pressing one hand upon her mouth, with the other he snatched her from the bed, and, before she became conscious of the harm that had befallen her, she was being borne swiftly through the cold night ⟶.

A caravan, standing upon the outskirts of the fair, was reached at the moment the canvas began to blaze.

It was then Lily began to shake off the deadly fear which was so strong upon her, and as her eyes met the dark features of her abductor, she tried to remove the heavy hand from her mouth.

"Quiet!" growled the ruffian, "or I'll choke you!"

The cry that came to her lips died ere it found utterance, and, every limb trembling with fear, she gazed helplessly at the dark, stern face and savagely gleaming eyes.

Men, alarmed by the cry of fire which rang out, rushed past the shivering girl and her captor.

Tinker Tom saw his danger, and running behind the caravan, placed the child upon the ground, and threw her clothing at her feet.

"Dress yourself," he said, and attempt to move one step and I'll cut your throat."

She saw the moonbeams glimmer upon an open knife, and, though help was within reach of her voice, she was too much cowed to speak.

When the child had donned her clothes, Tinker Tom took her hand, and, dragging her tired limbs over the rough ground, the fair was soon left far behind.

Along the quiet country road he sped, until the delicate feet refused to do their office.

Tinker Tom threw her across his shoulders, and as the sun began to dispel the morning mists he knocked loudly at the door of a quiet roadside public-house.

Here they remained until night again came upon the earth. Then the journey was resumed: the gipsy savage, silent, and sullen; the child pale as a spectre, and praying that death would relieve her from the grasp of her abductor.

So the journey continued until they reached London—hiding while the blessed sunshine gladdened the earth, and travelling when the night-loving bat and owl were on the wing.

In the upper room of a low water-side public-house Tinker Tom determined to stay until all possibility of being overtaken should have passed away.

Here the ruffian, gloating over his captive, indulged freely in the use of ardent spirits.

Here the poor child would cower in a remote corner of the dingy room, and with distended eyes watch the man as, overcome by drink, his head fell forward and his eyes seemed closed with sleep.

It was then the sudden thought of liberty came to the child's mind, and stealing quietly across the room she tried to open the door.

It was locked!

Lily clasped her hands in mute anguish, and, losing her heart, wept bitter tears.

Hark! what is that sound which causes her to raise her head and run eagerly to the window?

It is a long way off, but the well-known music which had so oft occupied the movements of her tiny feet was near, and with it she knew came help and her release from the power of her savage guardian.

Tinker Tom heard the sound, and unclosing his heavy eyes he glared towards the pale, frightened captive.

"Come away from the window," he said, his voice thick and scarcely distinguishable from the effect of his deep potations; "come away—do you hear?"

He followed the command with an oath which sent Lily cowering and shivering back to her murky corner.

By the time she had seated herself upon the little three-legged stool the beating of the well-known parchment had ceased, and she was again left to wonder what her fate would be should her friends not come.

* * * * * * *

"I'm nearly tired of this, Jack," said Long Bob, as they were putting their coats on after a very unsuccessful pitch; "here we have been up and down these streets and not taken a penny."

"I am tired," said Jack, "but if the woman spoke the truth we may yet come upon the place where Tinker Tom has taken Lily."

"Don't believe a word," growled Long Bob; "what did she know about it? It's my opinion he's made for the country, not come this way at all. What do you think, old un?"

"I don't know," answered Pipes, "what to think; we must have been pretty close on him all the way, but as to finding 'em here down any of these streets, why——"

"You knows nothing about it, you shadder," said Drum; "the old woman said she'd seen a man and a little girl go past the corner of this 'ere street."

"Well, that's nothing, there's plenty——"

"Lots of your jaw, so shut up until I've finished. Rats afore mice any day."

Pipes wiped his mouth with the old article, and muttered—

"Yes, and a good fat rat you is."

"Then," Drum continued, "when I asked all along each side of the way, nobody hadn't seen 'em pass out at t'other end."

"Then," said Long Bob, "the case is just this—if they have not gone away in the night, they are in one of these houses."

"That's just it," assented Drum, "but how is we to find out which is the house?"

"This is my idea," said Long Bob; "we can make several pitches here, and as the houses ain't very high, we can do a pyramid, and Jack will be able to look through the first floor windows."

"You won't be high enough," whispered Pipes, "you wants another."

Long Bob measured the distance with his eye, and found Pipes was quite correct.

"There's only one way to do it, Drum."

"Which way is that, Bob?"

"You must give your instrument to Pipes, and let him do the two."

"Well?"

"Then off with your coat and tile, and do the bottom in the pyramid."

"Do—do the what?" said Big Drum, aghast. "Me do the pyr-a-mid?"

"Now, look here, old un, it's no use being obstinate, so you'll have to do it."

"Shall I?"

"Well," Bob said, "if you don't, why I shall know that you don't care much for poor little Lily."

"Don't I? Quite as much as any of you."

"Yet you won't do this little thing for us."

"Why don't you ask Pipes?"

"Well," Long Bob said, "do you want us to be taken up for manslaughter?"

"We ain't as heavy as all that."

"No, Drum; but you must remember that Pipes is so thin that he will be sure to break in two, and there would be an end to the company."

Drum rubbed his nose reflectively.

He would have done anything to have rescued the child from the gipsy—that is, anything reasonable.

But this, Drum thought, was too much, and for a time his insulted dignity would not allow him to listen calmly to Long Bob's proposition.

Jack Lennox came beside his stout friend, and placing his small hand upon Drum's wrist, looked up and said—

"Won't you do it, Drum, just for once? —it's our only chance to find poor Lily."

Drum looked at the pleading face, wavered, and finally gave way with the words—

"Well, I will, Jack, but it's only for this once—mind that!"

So Drum took off his coat and hat, and Pipes, with a ghastly grin, suspended the instrument around his neck, and waited to begin.

"Go on," growled Drum, "if you has the two instruments, use 'em."

Pipes did so, and, resigned by the dulcet strains, Long Bob scrambled upon Drum's

ulders, then, lowering his hands, assisted
ack to ascend.

Several false notes were made by Pipes as
e joyfully watched the tribulation that had
allen upon his friend.

The memory of his own sufferings when
e had appeared as Jack-in-the-green should
ave made him more merciful ; but, strange
o say, the contrary effect was produced.

He beheld with glee Big Drum waddle
cross the street, and blew a louder note
on the mouth-organ when he saw the
adway had been recently repaired with
sh granite.

Nice three-cornered pieces, each piece of
edle-like sharpness, suggestive of more
an wonted suffering for those of tender feet.

Poor Drum ! he belonged to this class—
ough the soles of his boots were thick, he
lt the angles of the loose roadway as plainly
though his flesh were undefended.

Long Bob felt like a mountain upon the un-
ppy Drum's shoulders, and at every move-
ent made by Jack he swayed to and fro
th his load.

Human nature could not endure more than
certain amount of this ; and, as Drum was
human, he began to find that, unless the
per portion of the pyramid descended at
ce, he should be compelled to succumb to
s agony.

"Bob," he whispered, "do come down—I
n't stand it much longer."

The entreaty was lost upon R. J. in con-
quence of Jack at that moment uttering an
clamation of horror.

Long Bob upturned his face, and asked—

"What's the matter, Jack ?"

To Bob's dismay, the boy sprang from his
oulder, and, before our long friend could
ecover from the backward jerk, he came to
the ground, bringing the hapless Drum with
him.

Pipes stopped the orchestral performance
when this calamity took place, and stood,
with mouth agape, looking at his fallen companions.

Long Bob was the first to recover from
his fall, and, assisting Drum to rise, he exclaimed—

"Jack's gone !"

"What ?"

"Jack's gone—jumped off my shoulders,
and bolted through that window."

"Then," said Drum, "she are there, and
I—what ! the Buffler !"

Pipes here paused, and stood by his friend's
side, and face to face they stood with the
Buffler, who came upon the scene at the
same moment that Long Bob had beheld his
companion disappear through the window.

The Buffler cut their surprise very short
by saying—

"I'll explain everything by and by. Where
are the children ?"

"The child—children !" said Drum,
aghast. "What do you know of the
children ?"

"Everything," was the answer. "Were
they with your *troupe* ?"

"One," said Drum ; "but he's gone."

"Gone ! speak man, I am——"

"He's sloped through that window there."

"Then," said the Buffler, "we will follow
him."

CHAPTER XVIII.

AT THE MERCY OF TINKER TOM.

WHEN all hope had passed away from the
child's aching heart, the joyful sound which
indicated the proximity of her friends caused
her to spring to her feet, and in spite of the
ruffian's menacing look, she ran to the open
window.

Grinding his teeth with rage, Tinker Tom
seized a bottle that stood upon the table, and
leaning towards the child, said—

"Make the slightest noise, and I will
smash your skull with this !"

Lily retreated from the savage, and burst
into tears.

"Cry," he growled; "it will do you good;
keep it up—it will make an addition to the
noise your friends are making—Ah, I've
caught the cub as well !"

He sprang to his feet as Jack, with a
gladsome shout, jumped from Long Bob's
shoulders to the window sill.

A moment he stood to recover his balance,
and stepping lightly upon the table, said—

"Lily, dear Lily, you are saved !"

The boy had scarcely uttered these words,
when Tinker Tom sprang upon him—there
was a dull thud, as the ruffian's huge fist
came crashing upon Jack's forehead, and
vainly trying to grasp at the hand which
smote him, the boy fell to the ground, bereft
of sense or motion.

The house in which this scene took place
was one of the lowest of its class, a dirty
beer-house, frequented by the rough water-
side labourers, and kept by a man who
would have sold his own children, had such
an opportunity offered.

With this vagabond, Tinker Tom, anticipating a close pursuit and probable discovery, had made a bargain for the use of
one of the murky cellars beneath the house.

So, when the boy lay a huddled heap upon
the floor, he raised him with one hand, and,
throwing Jack's light form across his shoulder,
seized Lily by the hand, and hurried as
quickly as his wounded leg would permit
him down the rickety stairs.

The quick passage through the air somewhat revived Jack Lennox, and he began to struggle with his captor just as Tinker Tom kicked open the cellar door.

Once inside, the gipsy threw the boy from him, and, closing the door, folded his arms and gazed with savage triumph upon the young captives.

Though they were at the mercy of the pitiless wretch, Jack Lennox threw his arms around the girl, as though to shield her from him, and turning desperately upon their gaoler, said—

"Coward! your triumph will be but short. My companions will never leave this house till we are found."

"You think so," was the answer. "Do you see that spade?—before they shall reach this place I would kill you both and bury you. Look—the place is soft, and will not require much time to make a hole that will hide your bodies."

The girl clung closer to her companion, and a shiver passed over her frame as she looked from the rusty spade to the dark vengeful face of their captor.

Jack Lennox's brave little heart quailed not at this fearful threat; he did not believe the merciless gipsy would dare for his own sake proceed to such extremities.

He knew not the character of the man, or he would have been less hopeful; for the gipsy, in the dark mood that was upon him, would have slain them as remorselessly as he would have crushed out the life of a snared rabbit, or twisted the neck of a noisy fowl that resisted the hen-roost being pillaged by the midnight robber.

"You dare not kill us," he answered; "it would bring your neck to the halter, did you but attempt such a deed."

"I have done more than this in my time," was the sullen answer. "So beware, should your friends pass this door. The first cry you give will be the signal for your deaths."

"What have we done," Jack asked, "that you should seek to harm us? Let us go, and I'll promise that no one shall be the wiser."

"Let you go?" he answered; "let you go? when I have dogged you day after day, week after week. Let you go? No! no! no! You should know enough of the rules of our tribe to know how the Zingaris keep an oath made beneath the stars."

"What has this poor child done? She did not cause your companion to be transported. Was not the destruction of the earl's mansion and his death revenge enough? Let her go with those who are now seeking us, and I will return with you to the tribe."

"You shall both return to the tribe," he answered, "and, stretched upon the wheel, you will be repaid for shattering my leg."

"I did it but to save her," said Jack, "and I would do it again were the same need to present itself."

The gipsy's eyes blazed fiercely at the boy's bold words.

"You dare tell me this!"—he hissed—"tell me that you would raise your hand against me, and here alone in my power?"

"I would tell you so"—the boy's eyes sparkled as he spoke—"were your fingers entwined round my throat, and the words the last I uttered. Here, alone as we are, I tell you to beware what you are about, or you will suffer for this outrage—"

"Viper!" hissed Tinker Tom, between his clenched teeth; "another word, and I'll choke you!"

"Do your worst," said the boy, angrily; and, springing lightly across the cellar, he seized the spade, and, swinging it backwards, added—"stand from the door, or I'll cut you down, ruffian as you are!"

The heavy weapon described a swift circle, and had not Tinker Tom sprung nimbly aside he would have been seriously hurt; for the boy, driven to desperation at the thought of his friends leaving the house without discovering their hiding-place, seemed, for the moment, to possess the strength of a man.

The sharp corner of the iron blade sank deeply into the panel of the door, and Tinker Tom, with a howl like an enraged panther, sprang upon Lily's brave defender.

His superior weight bore the lad to the earth, and, as he pressed one knee upon the panting chest and entwined his fingers round the small throat, he hissed—

"Curse you, that blow shall be your last!"

Lily screamed aloud in her agony, for the boy's pale face was becoming of a dark red hue as the ruffian's fingers grew tighter and checked back the life current in Jack's veins.

But for that cry there would have been a fell murder in that murky chamber, for the lad's struggles to rise were becoming still, and his face, as the terrible sense of suffocation became stronger upon him, lost its identity, and carried an expression that was horridly grotesque.

While the echoes of her shrieks even yet seemed to cling to the dank walls, there came the sound of a well-known voice, then the door was burst in, and Tinker Tom, with a cry such as a tiger would have given had the brute been disturbed from its prey, turned and faced the deliverers.

*   *   *   *   *

Long Bob was the first to enter the "Waterman's Arms," the Buffler next, then Big Drum and his genteel friend—the two last much astonished at their old companion's appearance and the manner in which he stopped any questioning respecting their past connection.

Drum's wonder increased every step he followed the cool and somewhat commanding Buffler; and, glancing downward at his own clothes, he felt morally certain the contents of the lost cash-box had been expended in adorning the ungrateful Buffler's person.

"That's him," whispered Pipes to himself; "he slopes with two pun two and fourpence ha'penny, and before we asks him a word about it, he tells us to shut up. "I wonder," he added, "how he knew about us having the two kids with us? I allers said he was a knowing cove, and so he is—but the two pun two four and a half, vere's that gone to? I shall ask him if Drum don't."

Long Bob was too much concerned about his companion's disappearance to give a thought about the Buffler's sudden appearance; but with that instinctive perception which had been early developed in the rough school wherein he had been reared, R. J. saw that the Buffler was a man who could help them through the task they were upon.

"He's no street performer," was Bob's mental remark; "looks more like a peeler in disguise. If he is, so much the better for us."

They met the landlord of the "Waterman's Arms" emerging from a dusky den, called by courtesy the bar-parlour.

He gave a keen look at the private detective, and throwing open the tap-room door said—

"This way, gentlemen, this way."

"Stay," said John Harvey, placing his hand upon the landlord's shoulder.

The contact of the private detective's hand with the greasy coat-collar sent a thrill through the landlord's veins. He knew from experience the peculiar touch that signified the unpleasant companionship with the dreaded officers of the law.

There were countless acts upon the landlord's mind which merited a visit to one of her Majesty's prisons, and not knowing which of these had been discovered, a shivering seized his limbs.

The private detective saw the mistake the landlord had made, and, knowing the advantage he possessed, he said—

"Where is the boy that came into your house a few minutes since?"

"Boy!" reiterated the landlord; "I have not seen a boy."

This was the truth; and the Buffler, although he felt certain that Tinker Tom and the child were in the room when Jack entered, yet had no positive proof.

"I cannot," he thought, "frighten the fellow into an admission of the gipsy's presence here, so must manage to search the place for the boy."

"I'll tell you what, landlord," said Long Bob, slowly turning up his sleeves, "it's my opinion there was a gipsy fellow in that room with a little girl he stole from us; so you had better tell us where they are."

The landlord knew his guest was by this time safely hidden in the cellar, so, with an assumption of boldness he did not feel, he said—

"You are quite at liberty to search my house, gentlemen; I know nothing of gipsies or children being here."

"That's a lie," thought the Buffler, who watched the man's face as he spoke. Then aloud he added, "We intend to search for them, and if they are found you will suffer for aiding in the abduction of the child as well as other matters."

This was a random shot caused by the fellow's ill-disguised terror when they first entered.

The landlord evidently thought it the wisest course to conciliate the supposed policeman, so, calling him aside, he said—

"You are a detective, are you not?"

"Why?"

"Look here. It's no use denying it—you are."

"Well."

"Have you come here for anything else besides the child that has been stolen?"

"That will depend upon how much you may assist me to rescue her."

"Suppose I give you the direction where to find them, will you leave here without—without——"

"Taking you," Harvey said, supplying the words. "Tell me where they are, and for the present you will be safe."

The landlord breathed freely. He had a few days before purchased a quantity of valuable goods stolen from a vessel by the men employed in unloading her, and his guilty mind pointed out this as the cause of the detective's visit.

Finding that a betrayal of Tinker Tom would save him, he said—

"Go down those stairs, and directly opposite you will see a door; inside you will find those you seek."

John Harvey lowered his voice; then, joining the company, told them the intelligence he had gained.

"I cannot," he said, "interfere in the matter myself; therefore, to keep the landlord out of mischief, I will stay here until you return."

Long Bob went down the stairs three at once, closely followed by his companions.

When they had reached the bottom the

landlord asked the detective to step inside the bar-parlour.

"I would rather," he said, "you did so, for I do not wish my customers to see too much."

Harvey complied, and, taking a seat, waited impatiently for the return of his companions.

Scarcely had the trio reached the bottom of the steps when Lily's scream of fear was heard, and Big Drum, throwing himself against the door, burst it in.

He was the first inside the cellar, and placing the drum upon the ground, turned towards Tinker Tom, a stick in each hand—his warlike spirit aroused by the sight of Jack's peril.

Luckless Drum! He had not moved more than three paces from his instrument when Tinker Tom sprang to his feet and rushed upon our stout friend. The first blow Drum received knocked his hat over his eyes—the next caught him in the chest and sent him clean through the head of his beloved instrument.

Long Bob, in spite of his anger at the brutal outrage which they had arrived in time to prevent coming to a fatal result, could not forbear smiling at the ridiculous sight which poor Drum presented, as, poised in the shell of his damaged instrument, his hat over his eyes, and his arms hanging over each side, he gasped for breath.

Pipes, with a wise discretion, kept behind R. J.; and the latter, seeing he had a formidable antagonist, but not a whit afraid of the encounter, put himself in a posture of defence, and well stopping the gipsy's first blow, cried out—

"Come on, you skulking, cowardly hound; see if you can get me down as you did that poor little fellow—take that!"

He delivered such a facer that Tinker Tom, strong as he was, reeled back, his eyes flashing as though a thousand lights had been before him.

As far as strength went, Tinker Tom was much superior to his opponent.

But he wanted that activity and skill which Bob possessed. Could he have once closed with R. J. the fight would soon have been over; but our long, wiry friend, knowing this, kept his foe well at bay.

Slowly and cautiously he worked round the gipsy, and for every blow he received Tinker Tom received three in return.

"I shall blind him soon," Bob thought, "if my eye does not close up."

There was every probability of this occurring, as Bob, in the outset of the fight, received a blow over the left eye, and already a black circular mark began to appear and increase in colour every moment.

R. J. did not despair. He had also severely marked Tinker Tom's face, and every mad rush the gipsy made to close, Long Bob skilfully shot under his guard, and like lightning his fists played upon his opponent's face.

Tinker Tom's savage haste to grapple with his wiry foe soon rendered him breathless, and Long Bob, preserving his strength for a final effort, watched his opportunity to end the combat.

It came sooner than he expected. The gipsy, maddened by the severe punishment he had received, determined, in spite of R. J.'s science, to grapple and throw his antagonist.

Bob saw the intention, and as Tinker Tom came rushing upon him, he stepped aside and delivered a right-hander straight from the shoulder.

The blow struck the spot R. J. had long been trying to reach—behind the gipsy's ear—and as though he had been felled by a pole-axe Tinker Tom dropped to the ground.

"Had enough?" R. J. asked, as he floored the baffled ruffian; "there's plenty left."

"Hooray!" shouted Pipes, rushing from his corner, armed with the spade, "shall I smash him, Bob?"

The Buffler came to the door as Pipes planted one foot upon the gipsy's breast; and fearing Pipes would use the edge of the spade (he little knew our thin friend's valour had not appeared until Bob floored his opponent), he called out—

"Don't strike him; I have sent for a policeman."

Tinker Tom tried to rise, and Pipes beat a hasty retreat.

"Lie still," said Bob, clenching his hands, "or I will knock you down as fast as you can rise."

The Buffler soon relieved Drum from his uncomfortable position, and the constable appearing upon the scene, took charge of the gipsy, and marched him from the "Waterman's Arms."

The excitement beginning to die away, Long Bob looked round for the children. John Harvey answered his inquiring glance by saying—

"When they came upstairs I sent the boy for a constable; the girl, I expect, went with him."

"But," Bob said, "they ought to be back before this."

"I expect they are upstairs waiting for us."

"Of course they are," said Bob, tenderly feeling his damaged eye; "suppose we leave this cheerful spot?"

Poor Drum was the last to ascend. The damages he had received were to him infinitely worse than any bodily punishment.

His renowned hat was like the bellows of

BIG DRUM, PIPES, AND LONG BOB, HAVE AN INTERVIEW WITH THE BENCH.

a concertina in appearance, and one head of his drum was ruined for ever.

When they reached the bar, the landlord, in answer to R. J.'s inquiries, told him that the children had not returned since they went for the police officer.

The Buffler uttered a cry of alarm—a cry that was repeated by those who had come so bravely to the rescue; and like madmen they rushed outside.

The street was deserted, and like a thunderbolt the truth came upon them that the children had fallen into a fresh danger.

No one had seen them leave the house, and, not knowing which way to begin their search, the party slowly and sorrowfully left the "Waterman" public-house, their hearts heavy with apprehension for their little friends' safety.

CHAPTER XIX.

A CHANGE OF FORTUNE.

WHEN Jack Lennox was released from the brutal grasp of Tinker Tom, he seized Lily's hand and fled from the cellar.

At the top of the steps he was met by John Harvey, and desired by him to fetch a constable.

Scarcely understanding the words addressed to him, the boy passed through the door, as the private detective descended the steps.

A few paces from the "Waterman's Arms" he met a police officer, and Lily, running eagerly forward, said—

"Pray go and save Bob; they will kill him!"

The officer looked puzzled at the child's strange words, and was about to ask their meaning, when Jack said—

"Go to that public-house. He is there."

These words were scarcely more intelligible than Lily had used, but the officer, gleaning sufficient information that told he was wanted at the disreputable beer-shop, left the children and ran towards the house.

Poor Jack, his brain in a whirl, and his senses confused by the late brutal treatment he had received, knew not what he did.

Still retaining his grasp of Lily's hand, he staggered more than walked from the "Waterman's Arms."

The street was but a little distance from the main road, and when in the busy thoroughfare, the noise of the heavy vehicles suddenly recalled his scattered senses.

He put his hand to his thrilling forehead, and, turning to retrace his steps, said—

"We must go back, Lil—I did not mean to—to——"

Lily uttered a cry of alarm as her companion suddenly released her hand, then

reeled backward, and fell prone upon the pavement.

The excitement he had felt for a time subdued his physical agony, but as that left him, he felt the effects of the ruffianly ill-usage, and the blood rushing in a volume to his head deprived him of sense or motion.

A few seconds sufficed to collect a crowd, and they looked pityingly at the pale, beautiful child, as she raised the boy's head and wept bitter tears of anguish at this fresh misfortune.

"Is he in a fit?" asked a puny gentleman, pushing rudely through the crowd, "look up girl, and answer."

The child raised her tearful face at these words, and looked blankly, hopelessly, at her questioner. Her little heart was too full to speak.

"It's a dodge!" the puny gentleman said, looking round at the crowd for approval; "they ought to be given to the police!"

"Shame!" a sturdy mechanic said, as he placed his basket of tools upon the ground; "don't you see the boy's head is cut and bleeding!"

He went to Lily's assistance, and with his faded cotton handkerchief wiped the thin crimson streak from Jack's temple.

The crowd, as usual, easily led either for good or evil, began to give the puny gentleman a little of their mind; and a rosy-cheeked butcher's lad suggesting a bonneting for the old gentleman, the latter made the best of his way from the impending dangers.

A tall gentleman, attracted to the spot by the children's strange attire, uttered an exclamation of joy, and moving forward, placed his hand upon Lily's shoulder.

"Miss Lily," he said, "what is the matter?"

"Oh, Monsieur Latour," said the girl, for once glad to behold a face she had so thoroughly disliked, "I am so glad you have come. Pray take us back to Big Drum and Bob; poor Jack is so ill."

"Do you know these children, sir?" asked the mechanic, as he chafed the boy's hands.

"I do," said M. Jules; "if you will get me a cab I will take them away from this."

The man looked from the stylishly dressed Frenchman to the children, then went in search of a vehicle.

One was soon obtained, and with the mechanic's assistance the senseless boy was placed in the cab, and Lily, glad to escape from the crowd, followed.

M. Jules gave the man half-a-crown, and told the cabman to drive to the Strand.

The cab was scarcely out of sight when Big Drum, Pipes, Long Bob, and the private detective made their appearance.

John Harvey eagerly questioned all who came in his way respecting the children, and to his mortification discovered the cause of their disappearance.

"A gentleman," he asked, "put them in a cab, you say?"

"Yes sir."

"Can you describe him at all?"

"I didn't take particular notice of him, sir," was the reply, "but I think he must be a foreigner."

"The Frenchman!" muttered the agent; "this is indeed unfortunate—they have slipped through my fingers—which way did the cab go?"

"There, then turned to the left."

"Hansom!" Harvey called to a passing vehicle, and, jumping in, he added, "drive quickly; a four-wheeler has just turned the corner—a sovereign if you overtake it."

"Right, sir."

The small trap closed, and the hansom rolled away, much to the edification of Big Drum and his companions.

"Gone!" Pipes said, "gone afore I could ask him about the box!"

"We're ruined," said Drum, "my instrument broke, and the young uns gone—wot unfortunit wretches we is."

Long Bob thrust his hands into his pockets, and muttered—

"What next, I wonder? I wish we—hallo!"

The policeman who had taken Tinker Tom to the station placed his hand upon Bob's shoulder.

"Why didn't you come?" he said, "the inspector's waiting to take the charge."

"We've lost the young uns," Bob said, "that's why—but lead on, we are ready to prove everything."

So they went to the station-house, and after having the satisfaction of seeing the gipsy led away, the company went slowly towards Mrs. Smith's hospitable mansion with dejected steps.

When Jack Lennox returned to consciousness, he found himself lying upon a sofa, his head bandaged and very painful. Opening his eyes wide with astonishment he saw Lily sitting at a table examining a book of prints.

"Lil!"

The girl was by his side in an instant.

"Lil," he repeated, "where are we?"

"Hush!" she whispered, softly. "The doctor has been here; he said you were to be kept very quiet. So you must not talk—at least," she added, "not yet."

Jack raised himself upon his elbows, and looked strangely around the well-furnished room.

"Not speak?" he said. "Why am I not to speak?"

"It was the doctor's orders, dear Jack; he ought to know better than you or——"

"But," said the boy, impetuously, "I am not ill. Never mind the doctor; tell me how we came here."

"Mind," she said, not able to keep her promise with the medical man, "you must not tell the doctor, or he will not let us be together."

"I will not tell him a word, Lil."

"Very well; I will tell you all about it; but," she said, musingly, "it seems so strange that I can scarcely believe it myself."

"Believe what, Lil?"

"The sudden way in which we came her and——"

He uttered an exclamation of impatience, and checked the child's speech.

"Tell me, Lily, dear," Jack said; "this affair seems so strange, that I am lost in wonderment."

"Do you remember," she asked, "when you were about to return to Big Drum and Bob?"

Jack passed his hand over his brow, as he answered—

"Yes—yes; but something must have happened since then, for I remember nothing until I awoke here."

"Yes," she said, "something did happen, Jack. You were very ill, and fell down, and you looked so white that I thought you were dead."

"Poor Lil; you must have been frightened."

"I was, Jack, very. Well, a crowd gathered round; and had not Monsieur Latour come up at the moment, I'm sure I don't know what would have happened."

"Latour—the Frenchman that used to be at the Abbey?"

"Yes."

"Well, Lil, what did he do?"

"He was so kind," she said, enthusiastically; "kinder than I ever thought he could be. You know, Jack, I used to dislike him so when we were at the Abbey."

"Yes—yes; pray go on, Lil."

"Well, when he came to us, he sent for a cab, and brought us here."

"Strange," Jack thought, "this man should take such an interest in us."

It seemed as though the girl understood her companion's thoughts, for she added, quickly—

"When we came to this house, good Monsieur Latour sent the servant for a doctor, and I heard him say that he knew me under—under—let me see—yes, under better circumstances. The doctor said it was kind of Monsieur Latour to take us from the street; then, after he had looked at your head, he told me I must not disturb you."

"Did you hear him say what caused me to fall in the street?"

"I did, Jack; it was something about the blood being forced up in your head and flowing on your brain."

"That wretch nearly killed me, Lil—he did—but he cannot do any more harm now. The policeman, I hope, took him away—poor Drum, I saw him"—Jack, in spite of the pain he felt, could not help smiling—"doubled up in his instrument; poor old Pipes, too—I wonder when we shall see them again?"

Lily shook her head.

"I don't think we shall be with them any more. Are you glad, Jack?"

Before the boy could reply, the door softly opened, and Jules Latour, with the cat-like gait of yore, glided into the room.

He held out his hand to the boy, and in the blandest tone said—

"Ah! I see you are awake, my little friend. Do you feel better?"

"I do," Jack said, shaking hands with the Frenchman, "and very grateful to you, sir, for your kindness."

"Do not speak of that." Monsieur Jules said this as though his heart was brimful of disinterested philanthropy, and the fact of bringing two children to his handsomely furnished apartments was a matter of daily occurrence. "I am glad I met you when you were so bad—so glad."

Lily came forward, and, placing her hand upon the Frenchman's wrist, said—

"We ought to be glad, monsieur; what could we have done without you?"

"Ah! well, my little lady, we will say we are both glad. Poor little girl"—the hypocrite caressed her sunny hair—"my heart did ache when I saw you in that dress, for you know, Miss Lily, I felt that I ought to do something for you; and, if you will let me, I will, and for your brave young companion as well—for I do——"

A rap came to the door, and stayed M. Latour's speech.

"Come in," he said.

A smart servant-girl entered, and, gazing curiously at the children, said—

"The dressmaker, sir."

"Ah! thank you. Will you go with the servant, Miss Lily? You must leave off these clothes; they are not fit for you to wear."

"Oh, Monsieur Latour!" she began, and her blue eyes sparkled with delight. "Am I to——"

"You must not say one word, Miss Lily, but go and get all things that are required—tell her to go," he said, in an undertone to Jack, "for I want to talk to you, my young friend."

"Go with the servant, Lil," said the boy.

The child silently obeyed, and he was alone with the disinterested Monsieur Latour.

The Frenchman looked after the girl, and, shaking his head, remarked—

"She will be glad to leave off those tawdry clothes, I should think. Poor little Miss Lily, my heart did ache when I saw her!"

He was skilfully working upon the boy's most vulnerable point; yet Jack did not feel quite at ease respecting his friend's goodness of heart.

"He must have a motive in this," the boy thought; "yet I do not see that he can. Perhaps, after all, it is because he knew Lil when she was in the Abbey."

Satisfied with this reason for M. Jules' queer behaviour, the boy said—

"Yes, sir, she will, indeed, be glad to change that dress; for although she has gone through the hardship and misery incidental to a poor company of street performers, her heart was never in the business."

"I can understand that," said M. Jules Latour, "she was reared in too much luxury; but you, my young friend, how did you like it?"

"But little," Jack said, quickly, "but as it was all that stood between me and starvation, I was compelled to follow it, and shall, I suppose, until a change of fortune has taken place."

"The change has taken place," said the ex-valet, "if you like to accept it."

Jack's face wore a strangely puzzled look as he said—

"The change has taken place, if I will accept it?"

"Yes," M. Jules said; "and for the poor little girl's sake I should think you would not refuse Fortune's smile."

"I do not exactly understand," said Jack; "pray explain."

"It is very soon explained, my young friend. I can place you in a position that will make you rich to most people."

"If you mean," Jack said, "that I am to live with you and do nothing for a return, I do not think I can consent, for sooner than live upon the charity of others, I will remain a street performer all my life."

"Very well spoken," said M. Jules, with affected enthusiasm. "I admire you for those words; but I think, for poor Lily's sake, you should be glad of anything that will keep her from the life she has been compelled to follow lately."

"I could do much for Lily," said Jack, "and I should be happy were it in my power to save her from the wretched mode of gaining a livelihood we have been compelled to adopt."

"You can do so," said M. Jules ; "you can do more."

Jack looked at the speaker interrogatively.

"I mean it," M. Jules said ; "you can place your little companion in a position nearly as good as that which she formerly occupied."

"How—tell me how ?"

"At present," was the reply, "I cannot say more."

"I cannot bear to be kept in suspense ; if there is anything to tell me, why not do it now ?"

Monsieur Jules rubbed his hands softly, as he sat on the edge of the sofa, and as a cunning gleam shone in his eyes, he asked—

"Suppose any one could put you in possession of an estate worth four thousand pounds a year, what would you give the person out of it ?"

"Well," said Jack, smiling, "when such a thing comes to pass I shall be very generous."

"You do not think it possible, then ?"

"No," was the blunt answer.

"Well, we'll suppose such a thing possible ; now what do you think would be a fitting reward ?"

"Well," said Jack, laughing outright at what he thought an absurdity ; "I think I would give away half. But who could do this for me ?"

M. Jules gave a silent chuckle as he placed a clearly-written sheet of paper before the boy.

"There," he said, "put your name to that, and if I do not, in less than a month, put you in possession of an estate worth the sum I have mentioned, I will forfeit my life."

Jack Lennox read a few lines of the document, then, taking the proffered pen from M. Latour, he wrote his name at the bottom.

"The man must be mad," he thought. "They say you should always humour a madman ; so I have signed a paper binding me to pay him one thousand pounds a year."

M. Jules carefully blotted the signature, then, rising, said—

"This is good ; we have soon come to an understanding. Now, my young friend, get well as soon as possible, then we will begin the business."

"Mad as a March hare," Jack thought, "but quite harmless ;" then aloud—"I am quite well enough to do anything you may require."

He jumped from the sofa as he spoke, and Monsieur Jules, pointing to his flesh-coloured tights, said—

"Ah, I had forgotten. We must have a tailor for you ; then we will leave here, and go to another part of London."

Jack had no objection to the tailor, but, before he consented to leave their present abode, he said—

"What am I to do about my late companions ? They have been kind to me, and I should like to see them again."

"You will be rich soon," said M. Latour ; "then you can repay their kindness."

"And have them to see me ?"

"If you like."

"Very well," said Jack, fearing he could detect the gleam of insanity in M. Jules's eyes ; "be it so. Send for the tailor ; then we will leave here."

The next day M. Jules left his apartments, and took the children with him ; and when the cab which conveyed them stopped at their new residence, M. Jules looked up at the roof, and uttered a cry of horror.

"What's the matter?" the children asked, in a breath.

"Ruined !—ruined !" said the ex-valet, wringing his hands. "The valise and all the papers are gone !"

Leaving the astonished boy and his fair companion standing upon the doorstep, Latour jumped on the box, and urged the cabman to drive quickly back over the course he had traversed.

"Well," Jack said, "I expect, Lil, we shall soon have to return to Big Drum, for the Frenchman's malady is getting worse."

"He's not mad, Jack," she said. "Depend upon it, there is something more in this than you or I can understand."

The boy shook his head, and, opening the door of the house, they went inside.

CHAPTER XX.

BIG DRUM'S INTERVIEW WITH THE BENCH.

THE loss of Lily and Jack was a blow from which Big Drum and his companions could not easily recover.

Apart from the use they were in filling the at all times scanty exchequer, the trio were much attached to the children ; and with a dogged faithfulness they wandered about the great city in the hope of gleaning tidings of their little friends.

But as the days passed forward, this hope became fainter and fainter, until at last, after a long, wretched day, they returned to Mrs. Smith's—tired, hungry, and penniless.

They had tried several times to collect a few coppers by giving a performance, but the public did not seem to appreciate a representation where the orchestra exceeded the company.

"We can't live with Duke Humphrey

much longer, Drum," remarked Long Bob, as he stood gazing hopelessly upon the tops of smoke-begrimed chimney-pots; "and the public don't care about us now Jack and Lily are gone. Poor little things! I wonder what has become of them?"

"That's just it, Bob," said Drum. "I ain't thought about hunger, nor thirst, nor anything else when we had hopes of finding them; but now I feels as though a something was a gnawing away at my inside—it's horful!"

"Not had nothing since last night," said Pipes; "then we had only a thin rasher of bacon, biled with the kollyflower I got with our last penny."

"I wish," said Bob, "we had the same dose again to-night, for I feel reg'lar knocked up."

"It's no use giving in," Drum said, unloosing his necktie; let's go to roost, and see what to-morrow will bring us."

"Not much," said Bob, "I'm afraid; however, we may as well turn in, for after what Mrs. Smith said this morning, I don't think we shall have a place to put our heads in to-morrow night."

"What did she say, Bob?" asked Pipes. "I was thinking about asking her to lend us a shilling in the morning."

"No good, old un. I've tried. I went to her after I tried the chandler's shop, and she told me we had better find a fresh lodging; for she expected, now the little girl had gone, we shouldn't have money enough to pay rent."

"The old cat!" said Drum, savagely; "after the way I paid her up, to turn round upon us like that!"

"She's no worse than the chandler's shop man," whispered Pipes. "Not so bad, because we've dealt there reg'lar ever since——"

"I say!" Long Bob called out from beneath a mysterious-looking heap which he dignified by the term bed, "it won't do any good, you two sitting there croaking about our luck. Why don't you turn in? They ain't a bit worse than the rest of the world. They all do it when a fellow's down on his luck."

Drum and his companion turned in, and the tired trio were soon asleep—Drum to dream of showers of gold being heaped upon his head; Pipes to dream of roving at large in an immense cellar filled with barrels of the frothiest beer.

Long Bob's dream was yet more tantalizing. He thought himself seated at a sumptuous banquet, and every time he conveyed a luscious morsel to his lips, a demon, with a face not unlike Mrs. Smith's, whisked the delicacy from his fork and conveyed it to a capacious bag which hung by his side.

The three awoke early, and a consultation was held respecting the matutinal meal.

"We might raise something on the drum," said the owner of that unfortunate instrument, "if that gipsy fellow had not smashed the head in."

"Ah!" Long Bob exclaimed. "Lucky thought. This is the day we have to attend before the magistrate."

"So it is," said Drum. "P'raps he'll allow something for the damage the instrument received."

"Hope so," said Pipes. "Hope it'll be a suvrin at least."

"What time shall we go?" Drum asked; "'cos if we gets anything, I'd like to have it soon."

"Eleven o'clock's the time, Drum. So let's have another snooze; it will save us wearing out our toothpicks. Ugh!—how hungry I feel!"

"So am I," groaned Drum. "I wonder whether we shall have anything more to eat!"

Pipes covered his head with the bed-clothes, and groaned audibly.

The darkest hour comes before dawn; so it was with our poor friends.

At eleven the trio appeared before the magistrate, who had remanded Tinker Tom until the police had made a few enquiries respecting the gipsy's antecedents, and the active officer having found sufficient to help Tinker Tom in the attainment of a free passage to a convict settlement, the prisoner was placed in the dock.

The first witness examined was our stout friend, and his peculiar answers caused even the magistrate to turn aside his head to hide the laughter he could not control.

Before Drum stood the broken instrument, beside this the spade which had been found in the cellar.

"What do you know of this charge?" the magistrate asked, when Drum, after being duly sworn, stood fumbling the brim of his battered hat.

"I knows all about it, your wertchop."

"Let me hear your statement."

"Yes, your wertchop. Am I to begin at the fair, your wertchop, or only when we found out where he had taken the little girl?"

"The fair?" whispered the magistrate to a grave-looking man, who sat beneath the judicial seat, writing.

The grave party whispered a reply, and the magistrate, smiling at Drum's attitude, said—

"You had better do so."

"Very well, your wertchop. This is how it was: This here fellow as is looking at me as though he'd like to eat me with a grain of salt, come one night and set fire to our show." The clerk's pen went very fast over the paper; he was making a note for his superior's guidance.

"We knowed," Drum continued, "that he was arter the little girl, so we kept a sharp look-out arter her, but not sharp enough, your wertchop."

"So it appears."

"Well, when the fire broke out the little boy as we had with us went straight to where Lily slept, and when he got there she was gone."

"Where is the boy?" asked the magistrate. "You should have brought him with you."

"I wish we could, your wertchop, for, worse luck, he's gone, and the little girl too."

The magistrate leant over and whispered to his adviser—

"We cannot go on with the case if the prosecutrix does not appear."

The old gentleman at the lower table handed his superior a slip of paper, bearing the words—

"He has committed an assault upon these witnesses, and there are other charges against him."

The magistrate glanced at the paper, then crushed it in the palm of his hand.

"We cannot proceed further," he said, "with the charge of abduction, as the principal witness is not present."

Big Drum's face was a study, as he looked blankly at the magistrate and said—

"What! is he going to get off arter blacking Bob's eye and sp'iling my instrument?"

"You can proceed with the second charge."

"Yes, your wertchop." Then aside to Bob, "What does he mean?"

"The assault," was the answer. "Go on, Drum; tell him about the nose-ender you got in the cellar."

"Well, your wertchop, when we found the place where he had put the little girl, we goes down to the cellar and I sets my instrument down."

"Is that the instrument?"

"Yes, your wertchop, that's it; and no sooner did I put it down, than the prisoner turned round and let fly with both hands."

"Let fly?"

"Yes, your wertchop, hit me, your wertchop; one of his fists on my nose, and the other hit me in the chest, and before I knowed where I was, I found myself sticking in my drum."

He held it up, and showed the damage.

"That will do—you can stand down."

"Yes, your wertchop; but ain't I to have nothing for the hole he has made in it?"

"His worship," said one of the officers, "is waiting to hear the next witness."

Drum very reluctantly left the witness-box, and Long Bob took his place.

R. J. gave his evidence with great brevity, and wound up by calling the magistrate's attention to his yet discoloured eye.

Pipes was next examined, but his evidence was nipped in the bud, by the magistrate telling him to stand down.

Tinker Tom viewed the witnesses with a contemptuous smile upon his lips. He cared but little for the trifling punishment the bench could inflict for an assault, but when the magistrate asked if anything was known of the prisoner, his face became ghastly, and as his hands tightened upon the rail in front of him, he writhed with passion.

In answer to the magistrate's query, a constable said—

"The prisoner is connected with a gang of vagrants, who some time since set fire to Falconmere Abbey; and, if the information I have received is correct, he is the man we have long wanted. I will not detain your worship with details of his supposed crimes, but merely ask for a remand until we can supply the link that is missing in the chain of evidence."

Long Bob, with much inward satisfaction, beheld the gipsy conveyed to the cells by two gaolers.

Drum watched the proceedings with a puzzled expression upon his face. He had a vague idea that Tinker Tom could make reparation for the damage he had caused. When he saw him taken from the dock, he began to feel there was but little chance of raising a breakfast out of the broken drum.

Much to the astonishment of all present, he turned towards the magistrate, and said—

"If you please, your vurtchup, make him give me something for damaging my instrument. It won't sound now, your vurtchup, and when I carries it down the street, the boys shies stones in where the parchment is broken."

"I am very sorry, my man," was the magistrate's answer, "that it is out of my power to assist you."

"It's werry hard, your wertchop," said Drum; "all through that feller we ain't been able to give a performance—we can't do it without music, and one head won't do without the other, so we is got regularly hard up, and ain't took a copper this two days."

The magistrate hoped they would be more fortunate, and tried to get rid of his troublesome witness.

It was no use. Drum had a fixed idea that either the magistrate or Tinker Tom should make the damage good; and when his worship told him that Long Bob was infinitely worse off than himself, the stout one answered—

"He may be, your wertchop, but I can't see it."

"But his face is bruised by that ruffian."

"Yes, your wertchop, but the drum is broke. Bob's face 'ull get well, and no one ever heard of a drum healing up after one of the heads had been smashed in."

His worship had the greatest difficulty in restraining his laughter, and having several petty cases to hear, he ordered Drum to have two shillings from the poor-box.

Before the money was paid a tall, distinguished-looking man entered the court, and earnestly begged the magistrate to help him to gain possession of his children.

The trio opened their ears as the gentleman stated the case, and Drum became so interested that he quite forgot the money he was to receive.

The gentleman stated that he had not seen his children for many years, but through the agency of a private detective he had discovered their whereabouts, but ere they could be brought to him they fell into the hands of a Frenchman, and he, from some inexplicable cause, refused to give them up.

The magistrate pondered over this extraordinary statement, then asked—

"Do you know where the children are?"

"I do not," was the answer. "In escaping from a ruffian, who would have injured them, they fell into the power of this Jules Latour."

"I can only issue a warrant for the man's apprehension," said the magistrate. "Possibly I may then be able to compel him to deliver them up to you."

"Drum," whispered Long Bob, "did you hear what that swell said?"

"I did. We'll follow him when he goes out."

"Like wax we'll stick to him. Fancy, Drum, if he should turn out to be Jack's father!"

"Well, what if he does?"

"What if he does? You antediluvian duffer, it will be the making of us—that's what if he does!"

"Can't you two be quiet!" Pipes whispered. "He's going!"

The sorrow-stricken man, with bowed head, left the court, and Drum, throwing his instrument over his shoulder, closely followed.

They had gone some distance from the court-house before Drum remembered the money the magistrate had promised him. When this recollection flashed across his mind, he wheeled suddenly round, with the intention of speaking to Long Bob.

But a yell from Pipes caused him to stand petrified with astonishment—a state of mind which was not improved when the unfortunate genteel member of the company said—

"You ugly porpoise, I know you did that on purpose."

"Did what?" Drum asked, wistfully gazing at his companion. "What did I do?"

Pipes was standing with both hands pressed to the side of his head, and tears of pain stood in his eyes. He had good reason for this, for Drum, when he turned so sharply, struck the unfortunate Pipes with the damaged instrument with such force as to knock him backwards.

Poor old Pipes! he was trotting closely by the stout one's side, and, not anticipating such an astonishing hit, made sure, when the sharp edge of the instrument came against his face, that his skull was broken at the very least.

"Do! can't yer see?" and Pipes looked at the palm of his hand, as though expecting to see it crimson with blood. "Been and nearly knocked my brains out!"

"Brains," said Drum, contemptuously; "you'd better find 'em first."

Pipes muttered something which sounded like "Hard-hearted beast," and giving the drum plenty of room, toddled after his companions.

Long Bob, after indulging in a hearty laugh at Pipes' misfortunes, went forward, and overtook Captain Carlin.

Our elongated friend had a tolerable share of self-assurance, so, without any preface, he went into the thick of the business at once. Touching his cap respectfully, he said—

"I began pardon, sir."

The captain turned and gazed curiously at the figure by his side. R. J.'s appearance at the time was anything but prepossessing. One side of his face was yet discoloured, a ragged cap adorned his brows, his thin legs were covered by a pair of dirty cotton drawers (tights); to complete his somewhat peculiar attire, an old coat, quite large enough to fit Drum, depended in loose folds from his shoulders.

The captain's look of surprise Long Bob interpreted correctly, and before our hero's father could ask the meaning of this strange interruption, R. J. said—

"I know I'm not very fashionable, sir; but if you like to try me, I think you will find I can do more to find little Jack than the beak and all his warrants."

"Who are you, my good fellow?" the officer asked.

"I'm called Long Bob, sir; proper name, Robert Jawkins."

This intelligence was not sufficiently explanatory to the captain.

"Well," he asked, "what may be the nature of this offer you have made? Be kind enough to explain."

Long Bob, with great brevity, told the captain how he first became acquainted with the children, their connection with Drum's company, and Lily's abduction.

"This black eye, sir," he said, "I received from the gipsy when we found out where the young uns were stowed. When I heard you speak about the Frenchman, I knew you must mean that Jack and Lil were the children. Now, sir, don't you think I can be of some use to you?"

The captain reflected before he answered.

"This youth," he thought, "loves my boy. I noticed the husky voice and twitching lips as he spoke. Yes, I will trust him."

Long Bob awaited the captain's reply with feverish impatience. Poor fellow, he thought his appearance would deter the bronzed officer from accepting his offer, but when the answer came, his heart leapt for joy, and he could fain have wept.

"I will accept your proffered assistance," said Captain Carlin. "You know my boy, and, if my heart speaks truly, his companion is my daughter——"

"Your daughter, sir?—little Lily your daughter — Jack's sister. Well, I always thought there was a likeness between them, that I did."

"I am not certain that such good fortune is in store for me," was the sadly spoken reply; "suspicion and hope bid me think so. At any rate you will do your best. You know this Frenchman, I presume?"

"I do, sir; I have seen him once, and I should know him among a thousand."

"I am glad of that. We cannot arrange matters here; let us step inside this tavern;" looking towards Drum and his companion, "these men are your friends?"

"They are, sir."

"Bring them with you."

Pipes' mouth watered as he followed R. J. inside the public-house, and when they were seated in the parlour, his heart filled with joy at the sight of the foaming tankard, flanked by a new loaf and a goodly dish of cold meat.

CHAPTER XXI.

LONG BOB UPON THE TRAIL.

THE arrangements were soon completed, and when the captain left the house R. J. had a crisp bank-note in his pocket. Big Drum and his astonished friend were possessed of similar pieces of paper; for the bereaved father, though his sorrow was so great, forgot not those who had been kind to his homeless boy.

They sat long after their generous benefactor had gone. The task set before them was of more than ordinary difficulty, for the officer, in obedience to that instinct which prompted him to believe that Lily was his child, had told Drum and Pipes, if they could discover the tramps from whom she was taken by Earl Falconmere, their reward would exceed all that he had yet done for them.

He waited upon the chief of the private detectives, after leaving the trio, and found to his sorrow that the children had so unfortunately disappeared when tracked to their hiding-place by Nicholas Harvey.

"It is not often," said the chief, "that my men fail at the very moment of success; but in this instance the peculiar circumstances of the case were such as to exonerate him from all blame."

"I am aware of that. Have you been more successful with the inquiry respecting the girl?"

The chief's face brightened.

"We have," he said; "and I am happy to say that my suspicion has turned out correct."

"The child is my lost daughter?"

"Yes, this is the substance of my agent's report."

Opening a drawer in the writing-table, the chief took therefrom a book, and as the captain, with suppressed breathing, listened to his words, he read—

"'As per instructions I visited the various casual wards, and when I began to give up all hope of discovering the tramp from whom the child was taken, I learnt the following information:—

"'By describing the part of the country in which the Abbey is situate, and speaking of its owner, I attracted the notice of an ill-looking vagabond, who soon found an opportunity of joining in the conversation. He had visited the place I described, and amid the coarse jests of the assembled vagrants, told how he had robbed a lady on the road, not only of her purse, but of her child—'"

The listener sprang to his feet, and exclaimed—

"My poor Alicia! my poor wife!"

"I will not," said the detective, closing the book, "pain you with the details written here. I can supply the information in less time, and more compatibly with your feelings."

The listener silently acquiesced to this arrangement, and the chief resumed—

"My agent learnt that the child was not long in these wretches'—for there were two, a woman being with the fellow at the time—power, for when passing a large mansion the child saw a horseman coming towards them, and was rescued by him."

"That horseman was Earl Falconmere, my most pitiless foe."

"Strange," said the chief, "that Providence should have made him the guardian of your child."

"More than strange," was the answer; "but pray continue. I am anxious to hear the end."

"A meeting, apparently a chance one, took place the next day between my agent and the tramp; the natural result was an adjournment to a public-house; once there, the tramp's tongue became loosened, and he told his companion that among the valuables taken from the mother of the child was a gold chain and a cross, studded with precious stones."

"My gift to my ill-fated wife upon the anniversary of our marriage," said the officer, in a broken voice. "Little did I imagine, when I placed it around her neck, that it would be torn away by the hand of a common footpad. Did your agent glean any tidings of this?"

"He did. It appears the fellow was afraid to offer it for sale, and up to the time he entered the public-house with his supposed boon companion, had it around his neck."

"Ha!"

"I see you anticipate the sequel. The man I sent drugged the rascal, and here are the chain and cross; and from what I can judge it is worth an immense sum."

The soldier took it without a word, and pressed it to his lips, then, as the muscles of his face twitched convulsively, he placed it in his pocket-book, and said—

"There can be no doubt of the child's identity now."

"I am glad we have been successful so far, and hope ere long to repair the mistake made by the man when he suffered the children to fall into the Frenchman's hands."

"Tell me," said the captain, scarcely heeding the chief's words, "does not your agent incur the risk of being prosecuted for robbery?"

"With regard to the chain?"

"Yes."

The chief smilingly answered—

"Not the least risk. The fellow, for his own sake, will be quiet."

"I am glad to hear it. Give this to the man for the intelligence he has gleaned."

The chief glanced at the figures upon the bank-note, and said—

"You are too generous, sir."

Captain Carlin made an impatient gesture with his hand, then said—

"I trust soon to be made happy by the sight of my children. With your aid, and that of others, I have hit upon the Frenchman's track. I do not think he will escape us long."

"I hope not. The man Harvey is like a sleuth hound, and when once on the scent, he will run his game down."

They soon after parted, the lonely man to seek his cheerless abode, the detective chief to attend upon a veiled lady, who passed our hero's father upon the door-step.

*   *   *   *   *   *

"Madam," said the gentlemanly agent, when he had listened to his visitor's statement, "your case is not hopeless. I think I may safely assert that your husband and children still live."

"My husband!" she exclaimed, wildly. "Impossible! He died upon the battle-field."

"Permit me, madam, to correct you—he was wounded, carried off by the foe, and returned as slain by his friends."

"Can this be true?" She clasped her hands imploringly. "Oh Heaven! how much I have to thank thee for!"

"Quite true, lady. If you will leave your address, I will communicate with you when I discover the whereabouts of those you love."

She gave him a card, a coronet above the name engraved thereon, below this an address in pencil. Then, as the tears began to course down her cheeks, she rose, and left the office.

"A strange and complicated affair this," muttered the principal; "the strangest I ever had in my hands."

He watched the lady enter a brougham, and drive away; then closed the door, and soon became immersed in the perusal of a pile of letters.

It was, indeed, a strange case, though not stranger than many that are daily occurring in our midst.

*   *   *   *   *

"Now, Drum," said R. J., "I think the best thing we can do is to spend some of this money in togs—what do you say?"

"I think so, too. Eh, Pipes?"

"Yes," whispered the thin one; "but hadn't we better have a little drain more afore we goes?"

"Not a drop, you guzzling shadder," said Drum; "so get up, and let's toddle!"

They did so; and when they reached the street, Long Bob suggested a cab—a suggestion which was carried, and much to the edification of Mrs. Smith, her lodgers made their appearance in a four-wheeler.

If the good lady's surprise was great when she beheld this unexpected sight, it was greater when our long friend emerged from the house shortly after in well-ventilated apparel, and returned arrayed in a fashionable suit of clothes.

Wonders were never to cease, for, soon after this, a man wearing livery, and what Mrs. Smith termed a smoke-jack attached to his hat, brought a letter for Mr. Robert Jawkins.

The letter was from the captain, desiring R. J. to lose no time in setting forth upon his mission, and telling him that he had discovered the necessary information respecting the tramp who had possession of the little girl.

"You two won't be wanted," R. J. said, when he had finished reading the letter. "So the best thing for you to do is to get yourselves some togs while I'm out. After that, drink the captain's health."

"Yes," said Pipes, "that's the best. We'll drink the captain's health."

R. J. soon after left them to their by no means unpleasant task, and as he swaggered up the street, under the influence of his ready-made suit and the jingling cash in his pocket, he excited many envious remarks from the boys, who had been wont to chaff the professionals when returning from their daily toil.

"Vulgar young ruffians," soliloquized Bob. "I don't suppose they ever saw a gentleman down this street before."

It seemed not; for, ere our friend could emerge from the narrow turning, a ragged urchin yelled out—

"Yah!—yah! Ain't he grand since he went down Petticoat Lane. Yah! twig his tile!"

Outwardly our long friend gave no sign that his equanimity was disturbed, but in his heart he cherished a hope that the time would come when he should have that precious youth's right ear between his thumb and forefinger.

"That comes of living in such a low street," soliloquized Bob; "never mind, if I find the young uns, good bye to Mrs. Smith's sky parlour!"

Our friend, with great forethought, made his way to the spot from whence Jack Lennox had been taken by Monsieur Jules Latour.

"Now!" Long Bob thought, "the next thing will be to find the cab—a difficult thing, I know—still, it is to be got over—ah, of course, the Cabman's Club, that will be the place, and as I am pretty well off for coin, and cabby as a rule never refuses to drink, I shall not have much difficulty in making their acquaintance."

So to the cabmen's club-room Long Bob wended his way, and when he reached the beery, smoky den, he made the best use of his time, and by standing any number of "goes" of hot he soon became on a friendly footing with the man he sought.

While the astute Buffler was losing time going from cab rank to cab rank, to discover the vehicle which conveyed Jack and Lily to the Frenchman's apartments, our long friend was in close conversation with the man who had taken the children and Monsieur Jules Latour away.

R. J. left the smoky den much elevated; and tossing his hat in the air, he exclaimed—

"Hurrah!—Long Bob is on the trail!"

CHAPTER XXII.

THE FACE AT THE WINDOW.

WHILE Latour was gone in search of the missing cab, the children talked about the paper our hero had signed.

"I do not," Jack said, "feel that I have been doing right by signing that paper."

The girl, in her childish innocence, knew but little of the world's evil ways.

"Wrong!" she repeated, "why wrong?"

"I do not know," he said; "but still, I feel that it is so."

"Then I would try and get the paper," she said, "and burn it."

"I will," said the boy.

That night the paper was abstracted from Latour's valise; he had found it a few yards from the door, it having fallen from the roof of the cab.

Jack watched it burn, and when the tinder fell from his hand he crept into bed trembling, as though he had been guilty of a dreadful crime.

The Frenchman raged like a demon when he found the paper had been abstracted, and seizing the boy by the shoulder, he fiercely demanded—

"What have you done with that paper?"

"I have destroyed it," Jack replied, boldly; "I don't feel that I was doing right by putting my name there."

Latour spoke calmly, but it was the calmness which excessive rage can only give.

"If you do not," he said, "sign another, I will turn you out on the street—so make up your mind by to-morrow morning."

Jack Lennox pondered over the Frenchman's offer, and the result of this deliberation was a determination not to sign the paper.

The children talked over the matter—Lily, her heart filled with gratitude for Latour's kindness in rescuing them from the streets—Jack, thankful, yet his suspicions aroused respecting the disinterestedness of Latour's motives.

"I may be wrong," the boy said, "to refuse such a chance of becoming rich, but I shall do so, Lil, until he explains how he has it in his power to place me in such a position."

Lily wondered how her late patron's valet could have the disposal of so great a sum in his power.

"I don't," she said, "quite understand it, Jack; but he must be very rich to offer you such a lot of money every year—perhaps, after all, it is because he likes you, Jack."

The boy smiled bitterly, as he said—

"People nowadays, Lil, are not in the habit of giving strangers three thousand pounds a year because they like them—no, Lil, there is something wrong, or he would not want me to sign that paper."

"You know best, Jack," she said; "sooner than you should do anything wrong I would take off these fine clothes and go back to Big Drum and——"

The door opened and Latour entered, with his soft, cat-like tread. He darted a quick inquiring glance at the young pair, then, seating himself near our hero, he said—

"Well, my little friend, what do you think of the grand prospect I have offered to you?"

Jack made a gesture to Lily, who immediately left the room.

"I must," the boy said, "still decline it, monsieur. Thankful as I am for your kindness, I feel that I should be doing something wrong were I to do as you wish."

Latour's brow darkened, and he had much difficulty to restrain the angry reply that came to his lips. He did so; and, with his face wearing a smile, and his voice persuasive enough to shake a stronger resolution than Jack Lennox had made, he said—

"Something wrong? I wonder what you mean by that—how can you do something wrong?"

"I do not know," the boy answered, "yet I feel that it is so."

"Why—why—what makes you feel this?"

"The large amount of money and the necessity for me to sign a paper before you tell me how it is that you have the power to——"

Latour jumped from his seat and gave vent to an angry expletive.

"You want to know all this?" he said. "You want me to tell you everything? I will when you sign this paper."

"That," Jack said, "will never be unless I am assured that I am not wronging any one. Poor as I am, I would ten thousand times sooner go back to my hard life on the streets than be rich at the——"

"You shall!" Latour exclaimed savagely; "you shall, both of you, go—go as you came here—in rags, and—and——"

He paused. Rage choked his utterance, and for some moments he paced to and fro the room like a madman.

Jack Lennox had made a small bundle of his tumbler's dress, and during the time Latour was pacing backwards and forwards the boy began to divest himself of his new garments.

The Frenchman turned suddenly, and, snatching the small bundle from Jack's hand, threw it out of window.

"You shall not go back," he said, "to those people you like; *diable*, I will find some other place for you."

An angry spot came upon Jack's cheek as he tried to save the worn garments from being thrown through the window.

"By what right," he asked, "do you do this? I am now convinced that you have been trying to make me commit——"

"Silence!" roared M. Jules; "you are a fool, and stand in your own light; but I will find another, and he shall have your money—more, I will send you away to a monastery in France, where you will not interfere with me."

Jack Lennox looked strangely at the excited plotter.

"You dare not," he said; "I will claim the protection of the law."

"Dare not," hissed Latour; "you shall know when you are shut up in the walls of a monastery, and the girl you like so well shall go to a convent. We will see then what I dare do."

Latour left the room as the last word came from his lips, and to Jack's dismay he heard the key turned.

He was a prisoner, and although the window was but a few feet from the ground, he could not escape, for Latour had taken with him the clothes the boy had taken off preparatory to donning his old suit.

He stood in the centre of the room, lost in wonderment at this sudden change of fortune, and before he could form any plan to guide him, a tapping upon the window caused him to turn.

Was he dreaming? There was the well-known face of his companion in misery, Long Bob—not the ragged Long Bob of yore, but now somewhat showily dressed.

"Bob," he cried, running to the window and raising the lower sash, "I am so glad you have come; how did you find me?"

They shook hands, and Bob said—

"Pretty easy, young un. I found out the cabby who brought you here, and as I was walking past, taking stock of the place, I got this bundle slap against my head——"

"My clothes," Jack said joyfully; "Latour threw them through the window."

"Did he? I wish he had observed that I wore a new tile before he aimed at my head. Now, young un, as I've found you, where's Lily?"

"She's here."

"That's all right," said Bob; "get on your things; I shan't be long before I'm back."

"But, Bob, stay; I'll come with you. We can easily get Lil——"

"You'll stay where you are, young un—that was my orders, and when I return I will bring somebody that you will be glad to see.

THE RECOGNITION.

Shan't be long; good bye. You are a lucky fellow, Jack; so you will say soon."

Before the boy could reply, R. J. descended, by clutching at the thick ivy which covered the front of the house.

Long Bob hailed a hansom, and telling the man to drive like somebody unmentionable, he soon reached the captain's residence.

To the pompous hall porter R. J. said—

"Captain Carlin—he is here I suppose?"

The pampered menial surveyed Bob in a supercilious manner as he answered—

"Y-a-s, we have such a party staying at our hotel."

"I know that, Buttons," Bob said. "I asked you whether he was here."

The lacquey's dignity was hurt, and again surveying Bob, he was about to speak, when the captain hurriedly descended the stairs.

He had seen the cab stop at the door and R. J. alight, and impatient to learn the cause of our friend's arrival, came down in time to prevent an angry reply from the gentleman in plush and buttons.

A few words told the glad tidings, and when the cab reached Latour's lodgings the captain sent Long Bob to the Private Inquiry Office, to inform the chief that the missing children were found.

To R. J.'s surprise the grave-looking gentleman put on his hat, and entering the cab, told the driver to take them to a fashionable West-end street.

"He is not there," Bob said. He was anxious to return to his employer.

"I know that," was the reply, "but there is another person who is much interested in your little friends, who will join the party."

Long Bob wondered whom this could be, and his wonder increased when the cab stopped.

The joy of that meeting between the father and his long-lost children must be left to the imagination; it was a scene that pen could not faithfully describe.

Poor little Jack, when he found his gentle companion was his sister, wept with joy.

They had all suffered, but the reward was great—greater than their wildest dream could have portrayed.

8

CHAPTER XXIII.

CONCLUSION.

WITH an arm around each of his children, the happy father stood before the baffled plotter, and Latour, seeing the castle he had raised fall to the dust, sought to turn aside the captain's wrath, by telling him of the discovery he had made in the earl's chamber.

"I tried to find the young gentleman," he said, "after the fire, but did not do so until a few days since, and even had you not found him, I should have given him the papers which I found."

Our hero had told his father all that had passed between him and Latour, and thec aptain, too happy in his new-found joy, forgave the Frenchman for the deceit he had used, and when Latour left the room to fetch the papers relating to the Greyford property, the captain, in a low voice, said to his children—

"There is but one cloud upon our happiness—that, my dears, is the melancholy fate which befell your poor mother."

He had scarcely spoken, when a carriage stopped at the door, and soon after, the lady who had entered the Private Inquiry Office as the captain left came into the room.

She gave an hysterical cry when she beheld her husband and children, and the captain rushing towards her, cried out—

"Alicia!"

"Walter, my husband!"

They were locked in each other's arms, and the children, with wistful young eyes, gazed at their parents.

The embrace over—the embrace of those who had mourned for each other as dead—the lady came to her children, and holding them in a close embrace, wept tears of joy.

*   *   *   *   *   *

Where the blackened remains of Falconmere's proud towers stood, a splendid edifice was raised by the earl's daughter, and the workmen in clearing away the *débris* of the terrible conflagration, came upon the dead body of the proud Earl Herbert. He had lived for some days after the Abbey fell, for the spot where he was found had been to him a living tomb.

Across a low wall a mass of masonry had fallen, and in such a manner that it formed a perfect chamber.

Inside this the earl was imprisoned, and in the darkness of that fearful tomb he had written sufficient on a blank leaf of his pocket-book to restore his only child and her children to their heritage. He also implored her husband's forgiveness for persecuting them, and, when too late, saw the folly of giving way to the pride which had caused all their misery.

*   *   *   *   *   *

The mysterious reappearance of the Lady Alicia was soon explained.

She had sought her father when she believed her husband had fallen on the field of battle.

The proud man, enraged at her marriage had sworn to punish her. For this purpose he had her conveyed to a private madhouse and, filling a coffin with stones, had a mock funeral performed. He was ignorant of the children's existence—for the young mother dreading his vengeance, had left them with her maid.

It was this girl who was robbed by the tramps when on her way to the Abbey with the little girl.

She had started with the intention of trying to soften the earl's heart towards her mistress, whom she had not seen since the day she was conveyed to the asylum.

The loss of the child preyed upon her mind until her reason became unsettled, and blaming the earl for the misfortune that had befallen her, she suddenly took it in her head to personate her lost mistress, and for this purpose she took the boy by the hand and sought an interview with the earl. The result of that attempt drove her to desperation, and she plunged into the pool of water near the Abbey and died, as the condemned gipsy told the captain after his trial.

She had thought to carry out the deception by using the Lady Alicia's papers and jewels which had been left in her charge.

*   *   *   *   *   *

In the lower part of the new mansion three servants were seated—three privileged servants, to judge by the cosy room they had for their use.

One was a stout, pompous individual holding the position of butler in that vast establishment. The second was a gentleman of somewhat spare form. He held the office of steward, and, if all accounts are true, he looked well after the interests of his employer.

The third personage was a smartly-dressed young man—the young master's valet.

The butler helped his thin friend the steward to a glass of wine, and with much self-complacency remarked—

"Yes, Pipes, I always do say that it was a lucky day that young Master Walter met us.'

The steward sipped his wine like one who

understood the taste of a good rich old port, and answered—

"Yes, Drum, it was, and if he was here he'd say the same himself."

"Perhaps you'll explain," said the young master's valet, playing with his watch-chain; "really, I think the luck is all on the other side."

"Do you?" said the butler, who was rather severe; "that is where you are mistaken, Bob. Come, I'll put it to you this way. Do you think he would ever have got three such servants as we are, eh, unless he had been lucky enough to meet us when, along with Miss Alicia, he was OUT ON THE WORLD?"

THE END.